SECOND CHANCE MISTLETOE KISSES

THE CHRISTMAS ROMANCE COLLECTION

ANNE-MARIE MEYER

To all who believe that Christmas music can be played all year round.
You are my people.

CHAPTER ONE

Quinn stood in the ribbon aisle, staring at the piece of wrinkled paper in front of her. She was trying to make out the words that had been blotted out by Macie's black marker. Sure, it was an adorable drawing of a mom and daughter standing next to a Christmas tree their same size, but Macie had covered up the itemized list that Quinn had printed off.

Now, Quinn felt completely lost as she tried to make out the type of ribbon which she had noted would be best suited for a handmade bow. That was the last time she'd leave a piece of paper just laying around, waiting for her five-year-old's artwork.

"Mommy, let's get this one," Macie said as she walked up to the cart and threw a unicorn printed ribbon into the basket.

Quinn tried to catch it before it landed with a thud, but it was too late. She gave her daughter an exasperated look.

"We can't get that." She reached over the back of the cart, rose up onto her tip toes, and fished the ribbon out from the back. "Chardoney will have a conniption fit," she muttered under her breath.

She rolled her eyes at the thought of Mrs. Perfect. Perfect hair. Perfect body. Perfect house. Chardoney Suthers was the PTA president and snob of Middleton Elementary.

"Conniption fit. Chardoney," Macie repeated, giggling.

Quinn glanced over at Macie. "You can't say that around Serenity," Quinn said. That was the last thing she needed. Macie repeating the things she muttered under her breath to Chardoney's daughter.

Macie just continued repeating it as she walked up and down the aisle, running her fingers against the different sized spools of ribbon.

Quinn sighed and grabbed a couple spools of green velvet ribbon and threw them into her cart. She should have known better than to sign up to help with the holiday party. She wasn't crafty. She wasn't perfect. And she certainly didn't have the time to wrap the meticulous bows that she knew Chardoney wanted. But, Quinn's pride always seemed to get the best of her and now, she was stuck making these blasted bows.

And all the while, Chardoney acted as if that was the last thing Quinn was capable of.

"Come on, doll," Quinn said, nodding toward Macie and pushing the cart through to the next aisle.

After a thirty-minute trip through the store to find wire,

Quinn wheeled into the checkout. The woman behind the counter was incredibly slow as she scanned each item. Quinn stared at her, hoping that through sheer will, she could get this woman to move faster. It didn't work.

And, of course, Macie found the candy and starting putting them into the cart.

"Are you getting those?" the cashier asked.

Quinn shook her head. "Um, no. Sorry," she said, reaching into the basket and pulling them out at the protest of Macie.

"Not today," Quinn said, forcing a sweet smile to Macie when all she wanted to do was scream. She barely had enough in her account to cover the decorations she'd agreed to make, there was no way she had money to cover sweets too.

Macie threw herself onto the floor and began screaming. Quinn quickly paid and then half-dragged, half-carried Macie from the store.

The wind took her breath away as she stepped out into the freezing Montana air. She attempted to pull her coat closed around her, but with the bag and a limp Macie, she was unsuccessful.

"Little Miss, if you don't stand up right now, I'm taking away a present from under the tree."

Yeah, right. That wasn't a threat she'd follow through on, but she was desperate. After Ryan left, things had been tight. She was a single mom working as a bank teller, so money was a scarcity. The four measly presents at the bottom of the tree were the product of a lot of scrimping and saving.

Macie was going to get every one of them because those four measly presents were all she had. There were certain times in Quinn's life when she tried to will Santa to be real, and this was one of them.

That threat seemed to snap Macie momentarily from her fit. She straightened and allowed Quinn to guide her to the beat-up Ford truck. The truck was a gift from her father when her parents moved to sunny Florida to escape the freezing Montana winters.

Quinn would have escaped too, but with Ryan here, refusing to let her leave, Quinn was stuck.

After getting Macie into her seat and buckled, Quinn dumped the bag onto the cushion of the passenger seat and sprinted around to the driver's side. Just as she opened the door, a gust of wind picked up, causing her door to swing wide…and scraped the paint of the car parked too close to her.

She mumbled a few curse words under her breath as she shut her door and dipped down to see the damage. The shiny red paint now had a jagged line cutting right through it. And just her luck, it was a Jaguar.

There went her teeny, tiny savings.

"Excuse me," a deep voice said, coming up from behind her. "You scratched my car."

She closed her eyes for a moment before turning. She needed to prepare herself for the backlash that she was sure was coming. Forcing her sweetest smile, she faced the man, only to have her jaw drop.

Collin Stewart.

Frustration, anger, embarrassment…all the feelings that she associated with that man came rushing back through her. Why was he here? When did he get back? And why, oh why, did it have to be his car?

"Quinn?" he asked, leaning closer.

She pinched her lips together and glared. She couldn't help it. He'd broken her heart seven years ago and she still hadn't forgiven him. It wasn't because she was a spiteful person, he was just that awful.

But, her mom raised her to be polite and Collin looked as if he needed a response.

"Hey, Collin," she said as she tried to meet his gaze.

"Wha-what are you doing here?" he asked.

Why did he sound surprised? "I live here."

He glanced over at the Craft'n Stuff sign.

She sighed. "Well, not here here. I live in Middleton now." She folded her arms. "What are you doing here?"

He ran his hands through his thick, dark hair and dropped his gaze to the ground. A wave of worry washed over his features and for a moment, Quinn allowed herself to feel sorry for him. But only a moment.

"I, um…" He cleared his throat. "My grandma's not doing too well. I flew in from New York to spend the holidays with her."

Instantly, Quinn's heart squeezed. She knew that Ruby, Collin's grandmother, had been sick. She just didn't know it was that bad. She cursed her ridiculously busy life. She'd meant to go visit Ruby but things always seemed to get in the way.

She softened her expression and let a little smile form. It wasn't for him; it was for his grandmother.

"I'm sorry to hear that," she said. A gust of wind raced around her and she tucked her hands into her jacket, trying to contain her body heat.

Collin raised his gaze to study her. "Yeah. Thanks."

Silence fell around them. Snowflakes danced in the racing wind. The parking lot lights lit up the snow, making it feel calm. The darkness of the sky above them shimmered with stars.

Quinn's heart pounded at the memories of Collin which seemed to be trying to resurface. She'd loved him once. But that was a long time ago. A lot of things had changed.

A knock on the window behind her drew her attention over. Quinn's small face and big blue eyes peered out at them.

Macie.

Her daughter.

Collin's sudden reappearance caused her to momentarily forget the presence of her own child.

Grabbing the handle of the door, she turned to Collin who had a surprised expression on his face.

"I should really be going," she said as she pulled the handle and the door popped open.

Collin nodded and just as she slipped onto the seat and moved to close the door, he stuck his hand out to stop her.

Her stomach flipped as she glanced over at him. What was he doing?

"Your number," he said.

She swallowed. There was no way she thought that was a good idea. "I really don't think we should go down that path again," she whispered.

He studied her for a moment. His brows were furrowed and it looked as if he were trying to process what she was saying. Then he shook his head and chuckled. "Not for a date." Then he nodded toward his car. "The scratch?"

Realization screeched into her mind like a freshly scratched Jaguar. He didn't want to date her or talk to her. He wanted her contact information so he could send her the bill.

Her hands shook as she reached into her pocket and ripped Macie's artwork in half. After scribbling her number on it, she handed it over to him.

"I, um…" There was no way she wanted to tell him that she couldn't afford to pay for it—her pride had been stung one too many times with this man. Maybe, he'd be kind and bill her after the holidays. She could find some money then. "Can I pay for it after Christmas?"

Macie appeared next to her. "Who's this?" she asked.

Quinn glanced over at her daughter and then back to Collin. "Well, this is someone Mommy once knew."

Macie studied him and then shot her little arm forward with her hand stretched out. "Macie Humphries," she said.

From the corner of Quinn's eye, she saw Collin study her. Then he reached out his gloved hand in front of Quinn's chest and shook it. "Collin Stewart."

She eyed him. "Do you like marshmallows in your hot chocolate?"

He chuckled. Quinn moved to tell him that he didn't have to answer, but Collin said, "I'm a whipped cream kind of guy."

Macie gasped as a huge smile spread across her lips. "Me too," she squealed.

Quinn shushed her. "Go buckle up," she said, nodding toward her booster seat.

Macie sighed, but obeyed.

When Quinn turned back around, she saw Collin studying the piece of paper. She wished she could read his contemplative expression.

"I should go. I've got bows to make," she said, motioning toward the plastic bag on the seat next to her.

Collin glanced over and then nodded. He folded up her number and slipped it into his jacket pocket. "I'll call you later."

Quinn hated the fact that her heart picked up speed from those four little words. They didn't mean what they sounded like they meant. It must be her old feelings resurfacing. He was calling her to slap her with a big fat bill. That was all.

She started the engine and after a few gasping breaths, it roared to life. Collin stepped away from the door, allowing her to shut it.

She tried to ignore the fact that he was watching her as she checked over her shoulder and backed out of the parking spot. She wasn't sure what she was supposed to do, so she lifted her fingers up from the steering wheel in a sort of half wave.

Collin nodded.

Quinn shifted into first gear and took off.

Macie was bouncing in the backseat, singing softly to herself. After a few minutes of driving, she piped up, "I liked that man, Mommy. Are we going to see him again?"

Quinn's stomach twisted as she glanced in the rearview mirror at Macie. "Probably, honey," she said, breathing out the words.

Well, not probably. Most certainly. This was a small town. It was going to be hard to miss him. Plus, she owed him a new paint job. And from the look of his car and his clothes, things with Collin had stayed just as wealthy as she remembered.

At least her daughter didn't pick up on how hopeless she felt. Instead, Macie giggled and began blowing her warm breath on the window and tracing her fingers through it while whispering, "I hope so."

CHAPTER TWO

$\mathcal{C}$ollin stood outside of his grandmother's room. He took a deep breath as he crumpled the handles of the plastic bag in his hand which held the yarn that she'd asked him to get. What had seemed like a simple task, now had every part of his body discombobulated. His mind, heart, and emotions were a mess as he thought back over his interaction with Quinn.

Why did it have to happen that way? Why was she the one who scratched his car? He would have taken a belligerent drunk or a crabby, old lady over the girl he once loved.

He swallowed as he muscled down the emotions in his throat. Focusing on a love that once was, wasn't what was going to get him through this holiday season. He was here to see his grandmother and celebrate what might be one of her last Christmases. That was it.

He lifted his hand and knocked.

"Come in." Ruby's weak voice barely made its way through the mahogany door.

He turned the handle and stepped inside. "Hey, Grams," he said, holding up the plastic bag and nodding toward it.

Ruby was sitting next to the far picture window with the drapes drawn. There was a lamp next to her, casting soft light onto her weathered face. Her salt and peppered hair was pulled back into a bun at the base of her neck.

Her eyes brightened behind her spectacles as she waved him closer. "Thank you," she said as he set the bag into her lap. After rifling around in it, she gave him a smile. "This is perfect. Just what I needed."

Grateful that he didn't have to go back to Craft'n Stuff, Collin gave her a relieved smile. "Happy I could help."

Ruby retrieved a set of knitting needles from the large bag next to her and started pulling yarn from the ball. She eyed him and then nodded toward the chair.

"Why don't you join me?" she asked. The clicking of her needles filled the silent air. "Heaven knows that your father isn't much of a talker. He's been gone more than he's here since I moved in." She sighed, her face dropping from the weight she was carrying inside. In that one movement, Collin could just see what time had done to his grandmother.

A twinge of pain squeezed his chest at the thought of Ruby here all alone. So he gave her a soft smile and sat on the armchair across from her.

The silence deafened him as he glanced around. Ruby had something to do, but he had nothing. A stark contrast from his never-sleep lifestyle in New York City.

But that thought brought up more frustration than he wanted to deal with right now, so he released a shaky sigh of his own and leaned back, resting his hands on his thighs.

"What's with you?" Ruby asked, glancing up at him as the clicking of her needles continued.

Collin rolled his shoulders and shook his head. "Just antsy, I guess."

"You're too stimulated. All that working in the big city has forced you to forget what living a simple life does for a person." She gave him a smile which caused the wrinkles on the side of her lips to deepen. "It's good that you came home. Good for your soul." She paused and picked up a mug that Collin could only assume had her signature lavender tea in it.

She sipped it for a few seconds and then shook her head. "Cold." Reaching out, she rang the bell right next to her. Horace, the Stewart family's butler, appeared. He was dressed in a black suit with a tie. His white hair was gelled to the sides and his circular glasses sat perched on his nose.

"Yes, ma'am?"

Ruby gave Horace a curt look. "It's Ruby, for the one hundredth time. I'm your same age for heaven's sake."

Horace glanced over to Collin who just shrugged his shoulders. When his grandmother wanted something, or disliked something else, she let everyone around her know it.

"It's probably best to just go along," Collin said.

Horace sighed and parted his lips. "Yes, Ruby?"

Ruby grinned at him like she'd just won the lottery. Which was funny, because to Collin's father, Thomas, the lottery would be chump change. Too bad Thomas valued money over everything else. This was not the first Christmas Collin would spend with Ruby and only her. His father couldn't be bothered to leave his company to enjoy the holiday season.

"This tea is a touch cold. Be a dear and fill it for me and then come back and keep us company. I'm sure it's getting lonely in whatever room you're hiding in."

Horace glanced at her as he took the mug. She waved him on and he sighed as if he'd suddenly realized that there really was no way he was going to win this argument.

Once he was gone, Ruby glanced back at Collin. "Such a grump. We'll douse him with some Christmas spirit before this holiday is done," she said and then turned her focus back to her knitting.

Collin nodded. He glanced around his grandmother's room as her last statement rolled around in his mind. *Douse him with Christmas spirit.* Well, Christmas spirit was certainly lacking around here. His dad wasn't much into Christmas decorations.

And then, like a reflex, his thoughts returned to Quinn. His heart picked up speed as he thought about her and her daughter. How had he missed the fact that she'd had a kid? He knew she'd married Ryan very soon after high school. He'd walked in on her reception when he came back to get her. Leaving her had only been temporary. Apparently, Quinn decided to move on without him.

He had never liked Ryan. He was a jerk all through high school. What had Quinn seen in him? Collin was better in all aspects of life. Curiosity got the better of him. He hadn't seen a ring. Were they still married?

He glanced over at Ruby. She had to know.

She always knew.

"So, I saw Quinn today." He started slow and relaxed. No need to give his grandmother ideas when there shouldn't be.

Ruby glanced up at him and a small smile played on her wrinkled lips. "Oh you did, did you?"

He shot her a look. One, he hoped, said that he was not entertained by what she was implying. "Yes. She was buying something from that craft store you made me go to." He scrubbed his face. His grandmother's scrutiny was making him feel very uncomfortable.

She returned her gaze to her knitting and nodded. "So, how did the reunion go?"

"She scratched my car."

Ruby snorted. "Oh fate. You always surprise me."

Collin stared at his grandmother as she continued to have a side conversation with fate. When her voice trailed off, he cleared his throat. "Anyway, she has a daughter?"

Ruby glanced up and her gaze softened. "Macie? You saw her? She's beautiful, huh?" The clicking of the needles broke up the silence when she paused. "Poor Quinn has done so much more for that girl than her good for nothing father."

Grateful that Ruby was going to bring up Ryan, Collin sat back and allowed her to continue.

"You know he divorced her two years ago? Apparently, he had some side hussy that he was running away on weekends to see. Now, he's in Moose Falls with her, leaving Quinn here alone to raise Macie." Ruby's voice turned sour. "He won't let her leave the state so Quinn's stuck here."

A twinge of anger twisted in Collin's gut. He'd always hated Ryan growing up and when he found out that Quinn agreed to marry him, he'd almost gotten in his car and drove straight to Montana to stop the marriage. But his father intervened. Like he always did.

Ruby was no longer talking, so Collin glanced up to see her studying him. He furrowed his brow. "What?"

Ruby's lips tipped up into a smile as she shook her head. "Oh, nothing. You just have that look in your eye."

Collin relaxed his face. "I do?"

She nodded.

"What look is that?"

Ruby pinched her lips together as she continued knitting. She had a familiar look on her face. "Oh, it's just that look you get when you talk about Quinn. Or think about her."

His face burned at his grandmother's words. "And that look is?"

She met his gaze. "Regret."

The desire to pace rushed over him so he stood and began walking in front of the fire that burned in the fireplace along the far wall. He knew how Ruby felt about what had happened between the two of them, but he wasn't sure he wanted to hear it right now.

"What's she doing for the holiday?" Ruby nodded at Horace as he walked in. She reached up and took the mug of tea that he held out to her. She thanked him, insisted that he sit in the armchair next to her, and zeroed in on Collin again.

Secretly, he'd hoped that she would forget this conversation and move on.

But she looked as if she wanted him to continue so he sighed. "I'm not sure. We didn't talk that much."

Ruby narrowed her gaze. "With her parents gone and Ryan a flake, I'm guessing she has nowhere to go this Christmas."

"I'm not sure."

Ruby waved her hand at him. "Call her."

Collin stared at his grandmother. This was proof that she really was going crazy. "I'm not calling her." If only his voice sounded convincing. But it didn't, and from the look in Ruby's eye, she'd picked up on it.

"You are going to call her right now. She's alone this holiday season and she is practically family."

There was this sort of tug and pull going on inside of Collin from what his grandmother wasay. On one hand, he wanted to see Quinn again. On the other, he wasn't sure that was a good idea.

"Quinn isn't family," he said in a lame attempt to protect himself.

Ruby snorted. "And who's fault is that?"

Collin wanted to defend himself, but he knew what he'd done. He'd broken off their relationship to get out of this small town and make something of himself. To prove his worth to Quinn—a ridiculous reason. He could see that now. The demise of their relationship had been because of him. It was that simple. But that didn't mean he was going to put himself out there again. Seeing her on her wedding day had just about killed him.

Ruby held her ground as she kept her gaze on Collin. Realizing that there was no way he was going to win, he first glanced over at Horace who just shrugged and gave him an understanding look. Well, Horace wasn't going to do anything to help him so Collin sighed and pulled out that small piece of paper from his pocket.

The one he'd very neatly slipped in to keep it safe. After unfolding it, he took note of the fact that there were only two stick figures drawn next to the Christmas tree, and then searched for the number she'd scrawled across the paper.

It was a handwriting that he was all too familiar with.

His grandmother had gone back to knitting by the time he looked up. But he could tell by the way her head tipped toward him, she wanted to hear his conversation.

So, he punched in her number on his phone and then brought it up to his ear.

After a few rings, her sweet voice filled the silence.

"Ryan?"

Collin swallowed, as nerves clung to his throat. "Quinn?"

"Collin?"

A little voice piped up from the background. It was high and Collin couldn't quite understand what she was saying.

"Macie, calm down. I'm on the phone. I know, I know. It's going to be okay."

Collin could hear the panic in Quinn's voice. Something wasn't right.

"Hey, Collin? If you're calling about the car, this is a really bad time. I just got back to my place and there's been a fire." She let out a soft sob which squeezed his chest. "I just can't deal with that right now."

The urge to protect Quinn rushed through him. He stopped moving and straightened. There was a problem and he was going to find a solution. "Where are you? I'm coming to get you."

She sputtered for a moment. "I'm sure you have other things to do."

He shook his head even though he knew that she couldn't see. "It's what a friend would do." He winced as he waited for her response.

She was silent for a moment and then she sighed. "Fine."

After rattling off her address, which he scribbled on the piece of paper with her phone number, he had said he'd be right there and hung up.

Ruby gave him a quizzical look so he told her that he was going to help Quinn. A knowing smile passed over Ruby's lips as she murmured something about fate and waved him away.

After grabbing his coat and throwing on his shoes, he rushed out into the dark, cold snow, excitement and worry brewing in his stomach.

CHAPTER THREE

"*M*a'am? Ma'am?"

Quinn turned toward the voice which was calling out to her as she tucked her phone back into her purse. She saw a tall fireman walking toward her. He had his helmet on but his visor tipped up.

"Yes?" she squeaked and then cleared her throat. "I mean, yes?"

Macie was hugging her leg and peeking around at the fireman. Quinn could feel her fear as she stared up at the tall man. The smell of burnt wood and melted plastic filled the air.

By the time she'd pulled into the driveway, half of the house had been consumed with flames. The living room—including all four presents—and her bedroom were now a smoldering pile of ash. Someone must have seen the fire because the fire truck pulled in a few seconds later and had the house extinguished in no time at all.

Quinn tried to calm her nerves, but she couldn't help it. Her entire body was shaking. It must be the result of standing there, watching everything she owned burn to the ground.

"Do you have somewhere to go?" the fireman was asking her when she turned her attention back to him.

She furrowed her brow as she tried to piece together what he was saying. "Um, yeah, I think so."

Except she really didn't. Ryan hadn't answered her phone calls and her parents were unreachable. Right now, all she had was herself and Macie. Reaching down, she rested her hand on her daughter's head, hoping that she was bringing some sort of comfort to her little girl.

"Okay. The house is unlivable," the fireman continued.

Quinn just nodded. She knew what he meant, but the words just weren't registering. "So, when are we going to be able to go in?" She leaned in. "I have Christmas presents in there." Except she knew she didn't. There was no way her tree or presents survived the fire.

The fireman's eyes widened. "It's best to wait for everything to calm down. Perhaps tomorrow?"

Quinn stared at him. She blinked a few times. Just as she moved to speak, a man stepped up next to her.

"I'm here."

Collin's familiar voice washed over her. She knew she shouldn't be surprised to see him here, after all he did tell her he was coming, but she was surprised. History had shown her that Collin didn't always follow through on the things he promised.

"I—um, he said…" Realization washed over Quinn, causing her to stumble over her words. Tears pricked at her eyes. How was she going to fix what happened? There was no way she could afford to give Macie the lame Christmas she was planning before and now? There was nothing.

She sobbed and suddenly, Collin was wrapping his arms around her. Her breath caught in her throat at the familiarity that being held by him brought on.

"Hey, it's going to be okay," he said. The depth of his tone and feeling of his breath on her ear caused her to shiver.

Not wanting to try to dissect her reactions to him, Quinn just shook her head as her emotions exploded inside of her. She felt Macie tighten her grip on her leg.

"Mommy?"

Collin relaxed his grasp on her and stepped toward the fireman who looked a tad nervous. Quinn bent down and scooped up Macie, nuzzling her neck. She was grateful for the reprieve from Collin and reminded herself that all she needed was Macie and everything would be right in the world.

Macie pulled back and placed a hand on Quinn's cheeks. "It's going to be okay, Mommy. Santa knows where I am no matter what."

Except, there was nothing. No presents from Santa or presents from Quinn. All she had was the measly few hundred dollars in the bank and there was no way that was going to pay for a hotel and a Christmas her daughter deserved.

But she forced a smile and nodded as she leaned in and kissed Macie. "You're right," she said.

Collin shook hands with the fireman and turned. He had an uneasy expression on his face. Quinn studied him.

"Are you ready?" he asked.

Quinn furrowed her brow. "For what?"

He motioned toward the car. "You're staying with me until we can figure something out."

Macie giggled and pumped her fists in the air and then pushed on Quinn's chest to break the hold she had on her. "Put me down, Mommy," she exclaimed.

Out of instinct, Quinn lowered Macie to the ground. When she straightened, she met Collin's gaze. "We can't possibly stay with you." Unable to look him in the eye, she followed Macie with her gaze. Her daughter was making her way over to Collin's car and trying to open the doors.

Collin was studying her when she glanced back up. He shrugged. "It's just until you find a place to stay. I'm guessing you're exhausted and a rough night at a motel is the last thing you need."

She narrowed her eyes as she thought about what Collin was saying. There was some truth to his words. What she needed right now was a hot shower and a good night's sleep. Then she could focus on the fact that half of her house was gone and Christmas was just around the corner.

Macie must have figured out how to open his car door because the sound of it slamming drew her attention over. She studied her daughter who had climbed into the car and was bouncing up and down on the seats. She wanted to scold her daughter. Tell her that she already owed Collin so much for the scratch, the last thing she needed was to pay for new seat springs as well.

Just thinking about the money she didn't have caused an ulcer-like feeling to form in her stomach. She needed to get Macie and figure out what she was going to do. Zeroing in on the car, she made her way toward it only to be stopped.

Collin had reached out and wrapped his hand around her arm. "Hey. Wait," he said.

She paused, glancing behind her to see him smiling. Her resolve to keep him at a distance floundered when she met his intoxicating gaze. "What?" She snapped and then winced. She hadn't meant for it to come out as forceful as it had.

He dropped his hand and shrugged. "It's Christmas. One night isn't going to kill you. Plus, Ruby would love to see you."

Her stomach lightened at the thought of seeing Ruby again. "Okay. One night."

His smile lit up his face as he nodded. "Great. I'll drive."

Quinn studied his Jag and moved to protest but then chewed the inside of her cheek. "Okay. Let me get Quinn's booster seat."

She walked over to her truck and pulled open the door. It squeaked and groaned as she swung it wide. After removing her purse, the bag of ribbon-making items, and Quinn's booster seat, she climbed out. She pushed the passenger seat forward, grabbed the suitcase full of Macie's clothes which she had left in her truck after Ryan's last no-show, and slammed the door.

Once Macie was buckled, Quinn studied the back seat and then the passenger seat. What was she supposed to do? Sitting up front felt too personal so she moved to climb in next to Macie.

"Not going to sit up front?" Collin asked.

She yelped and glanced over. "Um, I wasn't—I can…" What the heck was she trying to say? Heat burned her cheeks as she got out and climbed into the front seat.

There was no way she wanted to be the person to bring up their history and how else would she explain not wanting to sit so close to him? If riding up front meant she didn't have to relive the pain by explaining herself, she'd do it. After all, that's what a normal adult who hadn't had their heart broken by the driver did.

After she was situated, Collin started the car up and pulled out of her driveway.

They rode in silence for ten seconds before Macie demanded that he play Christmas music.

Quinn hushed her and gave Collin an apologetic look. "Sorry. You don't have to play anything you don't want to."

Collin glanced in his rearview mirror and smiled. "Nonsense. I can play some Christmas music." After talking to his radio and telling it to play the latest kids' Christmas channel, *Silent Night* filled the air.

Macie relaxed in the back, her tiny voice singing along with the song. Quinn couldn't help but smile. Macie always reminded her of what Christmas was really about. Family. And having loved ones around her.

"Ruby's so excited to see you," Collin said.

Quinn turned to meet his gaze. "She is?"

Collin nodded. "I may have told her that you scratched my car."

Quinn winced. That's right. She'd scratched his car. She needed to remember that the scoreboard for who owed the other was stacked in his favor. "Right," she said, softly.

"It's okay," he said. His voice had softened and she could feel his gaze on her.

She swallowed, the weight of her situation bearing down on her. "It's not, but I appreciate you saying that."

The air grew quiet around them as no one spoke. Not able to handle the silence between them, Quinn spoke. "How's your grandma?"

"She's struggling. Her cancer is back. She doesn't talk about it much." She could hear the emotions that were stuck in his throat. "I wish my dad was around more. But, it doesn't seem like he's going to try to make it here for Christmas."

At the mention of his father, the air around them grew cold even though the heater was blasting hot air on them. Thomas Stewart. She swallowed as anger boiled up inside of her.

And then realization dawned on her and she instantly regretted getting into the car with Collin or agreeing to stay the night. "Is your grandmother staying with him?"

Collin's grip tightened on the steering wheel. "Yeah."

"Is that where we're going right now?" It was taking all her strength not to demand that Collin pull over on the side of the road and let her out. She was not going to stay at that man's house. Not after…

Collin glanced over at her. "He's not there. He's never there." He winced as he forced a smile. "It was a long time ago. Please."

She stared at him. How could he say those things? After what his father told him, he was willing to put her in this situation? It wasn't fair.

"Collin, he called me a tramp. A white trash nobody who was going to bring you down." And Collin listened to him. She fingered her buckle as the memory of standing there after prom, tears streaming down her face as Collin walked away.

And she was opening her heart up again to him. What was she doing? Man, she was desperate for willingly getting into his car.

And then a little cheer from the backseat brought her back to reality. Macie was sing-yelling *I saw Mommy Kissing Santa Claus* at the top of her lungs.

That's why she'd done this. All of her extra money needed to go to making this the best Christmas for Macie possible. If that meant saving money she'd otherwise spend on a motel, she'd do it. Even if it meant staying in that insufferable man's home.

So she forced herself to lean back in her chair and let her breath out. Plus, like Collin said, Mr. Stewart wasn't even home. And Ruby was. She liked Ruby. She could fake it for one night.

"I'm sorry, Quinn," Collin said, his voice low. She could see that his shoulders were tight like he was waiting for her to explode again.

She shook her head. "It's fine. It's for one night. I can do one night."

She folded her arms over her chest and turned her attention outside. She was going to survive. Right?

CHAPTER FOUR

*C*ollin winced as Quinn's words rushed through his mind. The memory of his dad standing there, demanding that he make a choice between Quinn or college was as fresh as the day it happened. It had been such an unfair and awful decision for his dad to ask him to make. Collin had thought he'd gotten over his choice, but he hadn't.

Everything that he'd tried to forget about Quinn came rushing back to him when he saw her standing in front of her burning house. She had looked so small and fragile with Macie. And he couldn't help himself, he wrapped her in his arms.

Which might have been a mistake, but it felt so good. So right.

Blast.

He pulled into the driveway and into the garage. After turning the engine off, he opened his door. Quinn was already out, running after Macie who was heading into the house.

"Macie, it's rude to just run into someone's house," Quinn said.

Collin shut his door and rounded the hood. Macie was starting to grow on him. Even though he knew very little about children, he was beginning to see the same stubbornness that Quinn had, in her daughter. It was one of the things that Collin had loved about Quinn.

"It's okay. I'm sure Horace will be excited to see her. I think he may have bought some cookies at the store."

Macie's eyes widened. "Cookies?"

When Quinn tensed, Collin glanced over at her. Maybe he shouldn't have offered her them. "If that's okay with your mom."

Macie turned, her hands clasped in a begging motion.

Quinn studied Macie and then sighed. "Fine. One. But then it's bed. Little girls turn into pumpkins if they stay up too late."

Macie scoffed as they both followed after Collin. He couldn't help the smile that played on his lips as he listened to them.

Once inside, he kicked off his shoes and Macie and Quinn did the same. He could hear Macie exhale as she glanced around. He studied her as she walked into the living room as she stared at the twenty-foot ceilings.

"This is the biggest house I ever saw," she said as she reached out both her arms and began to spin on the hardwood floor.

"Hey. Hey," Quinn said, moving to grab Macie who spun dangerously close to some expensive vase that Collin was pretty sure his dad cared nothing about.

"It's okay. She's fine," Collin said. He moved closer to her, trying to ignore how good it felt just to stand next to Quinn again. The memory of holding her in his arms washed over him. He peeked over at her, wondering if she was thinking about it too.

"It's only for a night," she whispered.

He leaned closer to her. "What?" Was she saying that to him or just reminding herself?

She pinched her lips together and shook her head. "Nothing. Sorry."

So it hadn't been for him. A twinge pulled at his heart as he thought about what that sentence meant. Quinn wanted to leave. She was here for one night only. He needed to remember that.

"Who's down there?" Ruby's voice called from the top of the stairs.

Instantly, Quinn's shoulders relaxed as she turned and made her way to the staircase. "Ruby?" she called up. "Macie, come here."

"Quinn?" Ruby appeared at the top step. She was in her wheelchair.

"Ruby!" Quinn exclaimed as she took the steps two at a time. Macie raced up the stairs after her mom. Not sure what to do, Collin stayed at the bottom. He didn't want to intrude on their reunion.

From where he stood, he could hear Ruby remark on

how big Macie had gotten and Quinn tell her about the house. Ruby consoled Quinn while stating that cookies were in order. She asked Horace to fetch some hot chocolate and the good cookies he always tried to hide, then offered a hot shower to Quinn.

Heat raced across Collin's skin as he leaned against the banister at the thought of Quinn staying the night. The feelings he'd tried so hard to bury weren't staying as dead as he wished they would. It had to be the fact that they had so much history. That was all.

"Collin, show Quinn to the guest room and help her settle in. I'm taking Macie to my room," Ruby demanded.

Knowing there was no way his grandmother was going to take a 'no', he said a quick "Yep," and took the stairs two at a time. By the time he got to the top, Quinn was the only one there.

He smiled over at her, but she looked uncertain. Realizing he wasn't even sure what to say, he waved for her to follow and led her down the hallway toward the guest room.

While he went inside, Quinn stayed in the doorway. Her eyes were wide as she glanced around. There was a king-sized bed against the far wall. A pair of french doors that led out to a private balcony were framed with floor-to-ceiling dark, grey drapes. Dark wood furniture pieces dotted the room. A Persian rug sat in the middle of the hardwood floors.

Collin was so used to this type of lifestyle that it had

become mundane to him. Just seeing it through Quinn's eyes caused him to pause.

"It's okay," he said, motioning her in.

Her gaze snapped over to him and she nodded as she stepped inside. Her cheeks flushed as she folded her arms over her chest. "Your dad always knew how to decorate," she said. Her voice sounded small and defeated.

Not wanting to talk about his dad or money, Collin led her into the bathroom. A double soaker tub was separate from the tall, walk in shower. Two sinks sat under a wall-sized mirror.

"Wow," Quinn breathed.

Collin wanted to stop her. He wanted to tell her that sure, these things were beautiful, but they didn't replace the very thing that was lacking in his life. Love. Someone who was there for him.

But he didn't. He was pretty sure complaining about the life he'd literally dumped her for was the last thing she wanted to hear. So he smiled and moved toward the shower.

"Pretty simple. You turn the nozzle and hot water comes out." He waved to the expensive soaps that his dad kept on hand. He tried not to wonder who they were for.

Quinn nodded. "Do you have a change of clothes?" she asked, pulling at her dark maroon turtleneck. He tried to ignore how different she looked now. Her teenage figure was replaced by a womanly one.

"You can borrow some of mine," he said before he thought about what he was saying.

Her eyes widened. He needed to back track.

"It's only me, Ruby, and Horace. I'm guessing you don't want to wear their clothes. So…" He shrugged.

She thought on that for a moment before nodding. "Okay. I guess I can work with that."

Ready to get out of the bathroom, he nodded and moved toward the door.

"Hey, Collin?"

He paused and turned to see that her forehead had creased. She was worried.

"Yeah?" he asked, the familiar ache to take away her pain stabbed at his chest.

"Watch over Macie, will you? She's all I have. I'd do anything for her."

The desire to protect Quinn's daughter rushed through him. He'd only spent such a short time with her, but that little girl was already starting to worm her way into his heart.

"I will."

She gave him a small smile and then nodded toward the door. "Can't do this with you in here."

Heat flushed his body so he turned and got out of there. Once the door was shut between them, he let out his breath. What had that been?

Instead of dwelling on his feelings, he made his way through her room and out to the hall. Once he located a pair of pajama bottoms and a t-shirt, he made his way back over to her room. He knocked a few times on the door, but when she didn't answer, he took that to mean that she was still in the shower.

He opened the door and stepped inside just as Quinn was stepping out of the bathroom. He froze. She had a towel wrapped around her body and one around her hair, covering her but hinting to what was underneath.

She yelped and he instantly covered his eyes. The image of that smooth skin across her clavicle and the length of her legs burned into his lids.

"I'm sorry," he mumbled. Then realizing that he was still holding the clothes, he held them out. "Here."

The pressure of the clothes left his hands.

"Thank you," she whispered.

Not sure what to do, he nodded and turned, focusing on the exit. Once he was on the other side, he leaned against the wall next to the door and took a deep breath. This was not good. Oh, this was not good.

How was he going to survive with Quinn here?

Needing a distraction, he made his way over to Ruby's room and walked inside. Macie and Ruby were busy dunking their cookies in their hot chocolate and talking. Macie had Ruby on the edge of her seat.

Collin wasn't sure what story Macie was telling, but it had his grandmother spellbound.

"And that's how Santa brings presents to you if you don't have a chimney," Macie finished.

Ruby leaned back and clapped her hands. "That's fascinating," she exclaimed.

Macie giggled and took another bite of her cookie. Then she paused and glanced around. "But you don't really have a lot of Christmas decorations up." She wrinkled her nose as she studied first Ruby then turned her gaze to Collin. "Why?"

Because Thomas Stewart hated anything sentimental, but Collin didn't think that Macie would understand that part. "Just haven't gotten around to decorating."

She studied the mantle hard. "Well, decorating is something mommy and me do." Then she leaned in. "She's not very good at it, so that's why I help."

"Hey," Quinn's low, playful voice said.

They turned and Collin instantly dropped his gaze. If seeing her in a towel did things to his insides, seeing her dressed in his clothes was worse. They clung to her very womanly figure. He swallowed and forced himself to bring his gaze back up.

She fidgeted a little when he glanced at her. Her hair was pulled back into a braid, accentuating the hollows of her neck. She held his gaze for a moment before dropping it to speak to Macie.

She wrapped her daughter into a hug. "What is this you're saying about me not being able to decorate?"

Macie giggled and stepped away from Quinn. "Mommy, you can't even make a bow for the dance." She wrinkled her nose. "You're kind of stinky at it."

Quinn dropped her jaw. Despite the fact that she was attempting to look shocked, Collin could tell that this wasn't brand new information. He raised his eyebrows, waiting for her to respond, but then she just shook her head.

"I think that's a fabulous idea," Ruby said.

All heads turned to study her. She had a smile on her face and a twinkle in her eye.

"What?" Macie asked, her voice a low whisper.

"I think that you and your mom are just what this house needs."

Macie's eyes widened. "You do?"

Ruby nodded. "We need you to help us find our Christmas spirit. It's missing!" Ruby clapped her hands and leaned into Macie.

"Where did it go?" Macie asked.

Ruby glanced up at Collin and gave him a small smile. "It disappeared a long time ago." Then she moved her attention back to Macie. "Think you can help us?"

Macie pursed her lips and furrowed her brow. Then after a few seconds she nodded. "I think I can help."

Ruby extended her hands out and motioned for Macie to come forward. They embraced. Just before they pulled away, Collin heard Ruby whisper, "You're going to do a great job."

Macie nodded and yawned. Quinn stepped forward and hoisted Macie up onto her hip. Collin wanted to do something. Say something, but Quinn just gave him a quick nod and stated that she was taking this pumpkin to bed.

Once they left, Collin glanced over to his grandmother who looked tired, but satisfied. Like she'd just finished some sinister work. He narrowed his eyes.

"What are you doing?" he asked.

She laughed and shook her head. "Sometimes, fate needs a little help." Then she shifted in her chair until she was sitting right at the edge. "Now, be a dear and help me to bed."

CHAPTER FIVE

The bright morning light shone in through the window and right onto Quinn. She squeezed her eyes shut, willing the drapes to close. She shifted, but nothing made a difference. Reaching her hand out, she felt for Macie.

Panic filled her chest when she came up empty handed.

"Macie?" she called out, sitting up and glancing around the room.

Her daughter was nowhere to be found. The door, however, was cracked open. Quinn was very sure that she had shut it the night before. Which meant her very precocious and rambunctious daughter was wandering Mr. Stewart's house alone.

Grabbing a small throw blanket from the end of the bed, she padded over to the door and peeked out.

The house was silent. Unlike her one bedroom rambler, which was no longer standing, this house was gigantic and for all she knew, her daughter was in a room in the south wing.

That's right. This house had wings.

She grumbled as she descended the staircase. There was no way she was ever going to find her daughter.

After the tenth room she checked, she breathed a sigh of relief when she heard voices coming from the kitchen. The shriek of laughter calmed her ragged nerves. Macie was in there. And from the low tones of the other voice, so was Collin.

Stilling her nerves, she paused outside the door and took a deep breath. Today, she was going to find an alternative place for her and Macie to stay while she figured out what she was going to do with her house. This whole thing with Collin was just going to be a blip on her radar.

Now that Macie was located, she needed to make a few phone calls before she took on the stress that being around Collin brought her. After a brief conversation with Bernie, the manager at the bank, he told her to take care of the house and he'd see her back at work after the holidays.

Grateful that he didn't demand that she come into work, she thanked him and moved on to calling Sandra, her best friend. That conversation took a tad longer. It involved calming her friend down after she said the words "house fire" and explaining why she didn't call Sandra for help.

As a flight attendant, Sandra was barely home. Plus, her small studio barely fit Sandra and her clothes, much less Quinn and Macie. Sandra poo-pooed her and then moved on to Collin, to which Quinn spent another ten minutes convincing her that there was nothing going on between the two of them.

Before Sandra agreed to bring her clothes, Quinn had to promise that if that status changed, Sandra would be the first to know. Once everything was taken care of, Quinn slipped her phone into her pocket and took a breath. Now it was time to face Collin.

After she gathered her courage, she stepped into the kitchen. Collin was standing next to the stove in a white shirt and pajama bottoms. He was listening to Macie chatter away as she sat on a barstool right next to him. Her hair was disheveled and sticking up everywhere.

As Quinn made her way farther into the room, they continued their conversation, neither of them glancing at her.

"…and that's why your thumb isn't a finger. Because it's smaller and shaped like a circle," Macie finished, smiling triumphantly over at Collin who was scraping eggs onto two plates.

"That is fascinating," Collin said as he picked up the two plates. He paused when he turned around, his gaze falling on Quinn. Her heart quickened as a soft smile spread over his lips. "Good morning."

"Mommy," Macie exclaimed as she jumped off the stool and rushed around the island. She threw her arms around Quinn's waist.

Out of instinct, Quinn picked her up and nuzzled her cheek. "You were supposed to wait for me," she said in a playful but firm tone.

Macie pulled back and placed her hands-on Quinn's cheeks. She pressed together causing Quinn's lips to puff out like a fish. "You were snoring, and I didn't want to wake you up."

Heat raced across Quinn's skin. She glanced over at Collin who was looking as if he was about to bust up laughing.

"I wasn't snoring," she said, hoping that Macie would drop the subject.

"Yeah, huh." Macie replied. She then tipped her head back and made a sound that rivaled a lawn mower.

Quinn brought her daughter over to the table and dumped her on the chair which Collin had pulled out. She motioned toward the eggs in front of Macie. "Eat."

Macie giggled and shifted on the chair until she was sitting on her knees. Then she grabbed a fork and started to eat.

Collin brought his plate of eggs over to the counter and set them down. "Sorry," he said, grabbing another plate from the cupboard and pushed half his eggs onto it.

Quinn wrapped her arms around her chest and shook her head. "It's okay. It's not your job to feed us."

He hesitated and glanced up at her. She melted a little under the intensity of his gaze. Then he shrugged and turned back to grab a fork and handed the plate to her.

"I know."

She reached out to grab it and brushed her fingers against his hand. Tingles rushed across her skin and she paused. It was

SECOND CHANCE MISTLETOE KISSES | 43

like his touch was so familiar and different at the same time. It took all her strength not to drop the plate. Their gazes locked onto each other for a moment. The intensity in his gaze took her breath away. What could he possibly be thinking?

Did she want to know?

Worry brewed in her stomach so she turned. Using both hands, she grabbed onto the plate and made her way to the table where she sat down next to Macie who was bouncing on her chair as she sang, *Jingle Bells*.

She smiled, grateful for the distraction Macie always brought.

"Are we going home today, Mommy?" Macie asked after shoving a forkful of eggs into her mouth. She blew eggs out with each word.

Quinn pressed her finger to her lips, hoping that Macie would understand. She didn't. "Not with your mouth full." Then she reached up and tucked a curl behind her ear. "Not today, honey. I think it's going to be a while before we get to go back."

Macie stabbed more eggs. "Good. I like it here. Collin said we could get a Christmas tree today." She grinned at Collin who'd remained in the kitchen, leaning against the counter while he ate his breakfast.

Quinn's gaze made its way over to him. He looked as if he were trying not to listen to their conversation, but so obviously was. "He said that?" she asked, turning back to study Macie. "Well, I think we've imposed on Mr. Stewart and his family enough." Plus, she wasn't sure what was happening with her reactions to him. It was probably best for them to leave.

Macie stuck out her bottom lip. "But they need a Christmas tree. And I'm the best picker." She dropped her fork and folded her arms over her chest.

Quinn sighed. Truth was, she really wasn't ready to get started on what her life was going to be like now that their house was uninhabitable. What did their future look like?

Maybe pushing off that responsibility until later this afternoon was best. So she smiled at Macie. "Fine. If Collin needs your help, I guess we can do that."

Macie cheered and pumped her fists in the air.

Suddenly, Collin appeared next to them. "You're okay with that?"

Not wanting to meet his gaze, Quinn focused on her eggs. "Yeah. If that's okay with you."

He was silent for a moment and fear crept into Quinn's heart. When she glanced over, she could see him smiling.

"It's perfect." Then he turned and began to rinse the dishes.

Quinn sat there, pushing her remaining breakfast around on her plate. What did that mean? And did she really want to know?

———

"This is the best one," Macie said as she stepped back from the large, blue spruce in front of her.

Quinn eyed the ragged, weather-worn tree in front of them. She glanced down at her daughter. "Really, Macie?"

Why had her daughter picked the tree in the back, hidden from sight? Half the needles were missing and there was a big brown spot on the side. "Don't you want one that looks a bit more...alive?" Quinn seriously doubted that this tree would last the three days until Christmas.

Macie set her jaw as she shook her head. "Nope. This is the one."

Quinn glanced over at Collin. She wanted to gauge his reaction to this. Would he just go along with it? After all, it definitely didn't fit his meticulously perfect life.

He had his eyes narrowed as he tipped his head to the side. "You really like this one?" he asked.

Quinn winced, bracing herself for his response.

He sighed and smiled. "It's perfect."

Quinn tried to hide her surprise as he stepped forward and pulled the tree off its stand. Together, Macie and Collin carried it over to the cashier.

"This one?" the owner of the lot asked.

Macie nodded.

"You know this one was in the back for a reason. It's dead. Headed to the chipper tonight."

Macie's eyes widened. "That's why I want it. It needs to live out its Christmas destiny." She leaned in. "I don't want it to be lonely."

Quinn's heart swelled at her daughter's words. Of course. She should have known. Macie was a collector of sorts. Always bringing lost souls into the house, begging Quinn to keep them.

Frogs, lizards, a stray dog. Quinn had to be firm but gentle to her soft-hearted daughter. She could barely afford to take care of the two of them, never mind the extra mouths Macie brought home.

The cashier eyed her and then nodded. "Sounds like a real Christmas thing to do."

Macie just smiled as the man grabbed the tree and pushed it through the netting. Once Collin gave his address to the delivery kid, they piled inside Collin's Jaguar.

As Collin pulled out of the parking lot, *We Wish You a Merry Christmas* played on the radio. For a moment, Quinn allowed herself to feel peace. Sure, this wasn't a perfect situation and heaven knew, she should probably try calling her insurance broker again to start discussing the plan for the house, but right now, she didn't want things to change. She wanted to keep reality as far away as possible.

"Do you have decorations?" Macie asked from the back seat.

Collin glanced into the rearview mirror. He furrowed his brow as he turned his attention back to the road. "I'm not sure. It's been a while since that house has seen a Christmas."

There was a sadness and longing in his voice that caused Quinn's ears to perk up. She wanted to ask him, even if she already knew the reason why. Thomas was not a sentimental man. Part of her had always wondered if Collin had picked up on that attitude as well.

He'd seemed so distant and cold when he broke her heart. For a very long time after that, she referred to him as the Cold-Hearted Dumper. Well, that was until she met and married Ryan—and maybe a few times after that.

But his treatment of Macie and herself seemed to contradict that thought. Plus, Ruby seemed to think he had a good heart and Quinn loved Ruby.

She sighed as she leaned her head back on the head rest. It hurt too much to try to think through all the things she thought she knew about Collin. Right now, he was defying all of those notions.

Her phone rang, cutting her from her reverie. She straightened and dug around in her pocket until she found it.

"Hello?" she asked.

"Miss Humphries?"

"Yes?"

"Patsy Reynolds. I'm with Montana Insurance. I'm returning your phone call."

Quinn swallowed. Nothing like reality smacking her in the face. "Yes. Thank you for calling me back."

"You said you had a house fire? Are you okay?"

She nodded and from the corner of her eye, she saw Collin glance toward her. Her cheeks heated from the concerned look in his eye. She couldn't think about what that meant. Not right now. "Yes. We're fine. We were out of the house when it happened."

Patsy blew out her breath. "I'm glad to hear it. Well, I'll

get started on the paperwork. Do you have a place to stay while we work this all out?"

Again, Quinn's gaze made its way over to Collin. She wondered if he had heard her question. Not sure what to say, she mumbled a "We should be fine for a short period of time."

Patsy was silent for a moment. "Since it's the holidays, things are going to run a bit slower. Is there any way you could get a more permanent situation? I mean, you can pay for a hotel, but I'm not sure how quickly they'll cut you a check. I know things can be tight around Christmas, so I just want you to be aware of how things work."

Quinn massaged her temple with her free hand. There was no way she could tie up what little money she had for any amount of time. "I can come up with something."

"Good. I can work with that. We'll need you to come up with a list of items that burned along with their monetary value. The faster you get that to us, the sooner we can cut the check. Also, you'll need to contact your bank to let them know what happened."

A weight rested on Quinn's chest. Sure, they had very little in terms of household items, but dealing with this made her feel completely alone. She had Macie, but there was no way her tiny daughter should have to worry about any of this.

After Patsy rattled off her email address, Quinn thanked her and told her that she would get the list to her as soon as possible and they said their goodbyes.

She slipped her phone into her purse and turned to see

SECOND CHANCE MISTLETOE KISSES | 49

Collin studying her again. He looked as if he had something to say. Like the words were resting on the tip of his tongue.

When she quirked an eyebrow, he spoke as if that were the key to his release.

"You don't have to go, you know that. Ruby would kill me if I let you to spend the holidays in a motel. You can stay as long as you need."

Quinn swallowed. She knew that was true. But she couldn't deal with that right now. She was pretty sure Collin's father didn't approve of her and if he showed up to her living there, he was sure to have words. But, right now, leaving didn't sound enjoyable either.

So she just smiled as she stared out the window. "I'll keep that in mind," she said.

Delay seemed like the best tactic. She'd face leaving, and the loneliness that brought, another time. Right now, she had a huge list of items to remember and Christmas to save.

CHAPTER SIX

Quinn was so quiet, it felt deafening. He'd only picked up on snippets from her conversation with someone named Patsy. He figured it was about the fire, but Quinn was shut up tighter than a ship.

Why wasn't she talking to him?

And then he'd told her that she could stay with him as long as she needed—but she'd seemed less than thrilled about that. Even though he was pretty sure his dad had something to do with this, he knew his father hated sentiment and would stay far away from his house during the holidays. But he doubted that comment would convince her. Great.

He kept trying to reach out to her, but she kept pulling back. Maybe he was the only one who was feeling anything. Perhaps, she'd moved on and he was the idiot who still longed to wrap her into his arms and hold her.

He squeezed the steering wheel as he stared at the road. Quinn sighed, and he glanced over at her.

He took a deep breath and decided it was probably best to just ask.

"Anything I can help with?" he asked as he pulled off the freeway and drove to the local holiday store.

Quinn glanced over at him and shook her head. "I…" She sighed again. He could just feel the stress that seemed to be tugging at her. "That was the insurance company. They want me to contact my bank and start making a list of items that were destroyed." She let out a soft laugh but it wasn't full of joy like her normal one. "They're assuming I had anything of value."

Collin's chest squeezed as he thought about her words. It couldn't be easy, being a single mom. "Ryan not around to help?" The question was out before he could stop himself.

Quinn shook her head, her fingers twisting the handle of her purse. "No. He's doing his own thing in Moose Falls." Her gaze shifted to the back seat. She leaned forward and dropped her voice. "I'm hoping he'll make it here for Christmas. Macie has a dance to go to for school and he promised to make it. But I'm not holding my breath."

Collin lifted his gaze to stare at Macie in the rearview mirror. She was singing softly as she twisted her hair around her finger. Frustration and anger rose up in his chest. What could Ryan possibly be doing that was more important that his daughter?

He pulled into the parking lot and into a space. After he turned the engine off, he pulled the keys from the ignition.

Quinn had her door open and was scolding Macie for taking off before a grownup was out.

Collin chuckled. This couldn't be the first time that they'd had this conversation. From the glassy look in Macie's eyes to the disgruntled expression of Quinn—they'd talked about this before.

Quinn and Collin walked side by side as they entered the holiday store. Large Christmas trees sat in the shop's windows sporting just about every ornament imaginable. He could hear the soft whispers of Macie as they stepped into the store.

It was like entering a Christmas world.

Macie had stopped and was staring around. She glanced back at Collin and a small smile spread across her lips. "This is where Santa lives," she said as she stepped up close to him.

The wideness of her eyes and the pureness of her joy tugged at his heart. Without thinking, he stooped down and picked her up so she could see the store better.

Macie didn't seem to mind. Instead, she wrapped her arms around his neck and pressed her cheek next to his.

"What do we get to buy?" she asked, turning to look him in the eyes.

He smiled. "Whatever you want."

Her eyebrows went up. "What?"

He set her down and grabbed a nearby basket. Suddenly, the wonder of this time of year seen through this tiny girl, had him wanting to decorate every inch of his father's cold

SECOND CHANCE MISTLETOE KISSES | 53

house. "Whatever you want. We are going to make this year the best year possible."

Her eyes were wide as she turned and picked up a package of Disney princess ornaments. "Like this?"

He smiled. "Of course." He waved toward the cart. "Get two."

Macie giggled as she dumped two into the basket. "This is amazing," she whispered.

Collin smiled as he followed after her.

"You don't have to do this," Quinn's voice spoke up from behind him.

He glanced behind him to see that Quinn was inches from him. His heart did a little flip when he noticed her proximity. "It's fine."

She raised her eyebrows. "You don't have to buy princess ornaments. I doubt they're a staple for fancy, rich bachelors." She nodded toward him.

At the mention of his relationship status, his stomach twisted. If only she knew how lonely and pathetic his life was, she wouldn't be saying that. "It's not all it's cracked up to be. Sometimes, a guy needs a little princess in his life."

He studied her, hoping she'd pick up on his meaning. Even though they were talking about the princess ornaments, he meant it to be so much more.

Quinn held his gaze for a moment and then reached out and patted the box. "Well, with two boxes of these, you'll have plenty of princesses in your life." Then she stepped forward to keep Macie from pulling the tinsel off one of the trees.

Collin stayed back, watching them. Being here with the two of them was filling a void inside of him. A void he didn't realize that he had until he was around the very people who could fill it.

After they filled his cart, Macie insisted that they had to buy a three-foot mechanical Santa. Quinn crouched down and told her that they didn't need it. Hating the tears that were forming on Macie's lids, Collin stooped down and studied her.

"Hey," he said, reaching out and touching her shoulder. "Do you really need that Santa?"

Macie sniffled and nodded. "Yes."

He studied her and then stood, grabbing the box and slipping it into the cart. Macie let out a cheer and suddenly the tears had disappeared.

Collin grabbed the now overflowing cart and wheeled it over to the cash register. He couldn't help the smile that played on his lips. It felt so good to make this little girl's Christmas.

He peeked over at Quinn to see what she was thinking. Was she grateful that he'd stopped a fit from happening? But, instead of a smiling, happy Quinn, he was met with her folded arms and set jaw.

He felt his excitement falter as he turned back toward the cashier and grabbed out his card. Once everything was paid for and stuffed into his trunk, they drove home in silence.

The more time Collin spent in the deafening quiet, the more he began to realize that he'd done something wrong. But for the life of him, he couldn't figure out what.

He pulled into the fourth garage stall and turned off the car. Macie was already out and running into the house.

Was it bad that he loved the fact that Macie felt so comfortable here that she could just go inside? The more he thought about it, no. It wasn't bad.

When he caught a glimpse of Quinn's furrowed brow, his excitement dropped. She looked less than thrilled.

"It's okay," he said as they both remained in the car. He could feel that Quinn had something she wanted to say, but wasn't saying it. Not sure if she got his meaning, he leaned closer. "She can go into the house by herself."

Quinn scoffed and shook her head. "Why did you do that?" she asked. Her voice was low and full of frustration.

He stared at her. "Do what?"

"Buy Macie that Santa."

Now he was confused. How was stopping Macie from throwing a fit a bad thing? "I wanted Macie to be happy."

Quinn turned and met his gaze. "Giving her everything she wants isn't the way to make her happy. She's always going to want more."

He could see the tears she was fighting to keep back. He'd really upset her and right now, he was so mad at himself for doing that.

Quinn reached up and massaged her temples. "Ryan used to do that—does that. He makes promises, buys her what she wants, but never follows through when it means the most." She turned to meet his gaze. "Macie needs to know what it means to wait. She can't be given everything all the time."

Collin turned to study the steering wheel. Wow. He hadn't meant to step on any toes. "I didn't know."

Quinn sighed, drawing his attention over. "I know. How could you?" From the corner of his eye, he saw her reach out and finger the door handle. "It's just, you're going to leave and I'm going to be the one left to pick up the pieces. Macie needs to learn to expect what I can give her." She waved toward the garage around her. "And this is not the life I can give her."

Collin furrowed his brow.

"You'll eventually leave and I'm pretty sure, Macie can't handle another heartbreak." She grabbed the handles of her purse and pushed open the door. "That's why we are leaving tonight."

His jaw dropped open as she slipped out of the car. He wanted to stop her. To tell her not to go. Now or later. He'd do better. Sure, he'd let his emotions dictate his actions earlier, but he'd keep that in check if it meant she and Macie would stay.

But she slammed the door and made her way into the house.

He sat, alone in his car with his purchases. A life that had once been his whole world felt so flat. If he couldn't offer Quinn or Macie money, then what could he give her? That was all that mattered to the Stewart family. He wasn't sure how to prove to Quinn that he was worth possibly taking a second chance on.

Feeling like a complete idiot, he pulled on the door handle with a bit too much gusto and got out. Frustration coursed through him as he made his way to the back and grabbed out the mound of bags that he'd shoved in there. He threaded his arm through the handles—he was going to carry every one of them in one trip.

After some maneuvering, he grabbed hold of the trunk and slammed it closed.

By the time he got into the house, Christmas music and the sweet smell of cookies filled the air. Ruby was down in the living room, marveling at the tree that Macie had picked out.

Collin glanced over at Horace who was wearing an apron. His normal proper attire was switched out for a red sweater and jeans. Collin stared at the butler he'd known his entire life. Never had he seen him so casual.

As if feeling Collin's stare, Horace turned around and gave him an exasperated look.

"Your grandmother," he said, waving toward his clothes.

Collin chuckled. He should have known.

"Princess ornaments?" Ruby said as Macie dragged her over to where he was standing.

Macie nodded and bounced a few times on her toes. "Yep. We got *two* boxes. You'll have to see them." She began to pull on the bags still attached to him.

Bending down, he slipped the handles off his arms and Macie began digging around in them.

"How about we eat lunch first?" Quinn said, stepping up to Macie.

Macie glanced over at her and shook her head. "I don't want to eat. I want to decorate."

The exasperated look that passed over Quinn's face tugged at Collin's heart. Before Macie could retort, Collin reached down and swung her up onto his shoulder like a sack of potatoes. "Come on. Little girls who don't eat lunch don't decorate trees. It's a Stewart family rule."

Macie giggled as she pushed her hand on his shoulder so she could look around. "But I'm not hungry," she whined.

He shrugged. "Too bad." When he reached the kitchen, he set her down on a bar stool and stepped back.

Horace had returned and was pulling out a bag of bread and peanut butter. "My famous peanut butter and jelly?"

Macie cheered and pulled her knees up under her so she could lean across the counter to help. Now that she was situated, Collin left the kitchen to find Quinn standing along the far wall of the living room looking very upset.

Worry rushed over Collin and he stepped up next to her. Had he made another mistake? He'd helped with Macie, right?

"Are you okay?" he asked.

Quinn dabbed at her eyes and straightened, giving him a weak smile. "Yes…" and then she blinked and slowly shook her head. "No. I just got a text from Ryan. He's not going to come down which means he's missing the dance." She sighed as a tear slipped down her cheek. "I don't know how to tell Macie. And with the house, I'm just not sure what to do anymore."

Without thinking, Collin reached out and pulled her

into a hug. She was tense at first and then slowly relaxed—which he was grateful for. Sure, he loved the way she felt pressed against him, but that's not why he was hugging her.

He wanted her to know that she wasn't alone. Even though she kept trying to pull away at every moment, he was here. Sure, he'd been a flake in the past, leaving her for some dream that he had chased, but that was over.

He was here now. And he'd be here for Quinn and her daughter until Quinn asked him to leave…and maybe a little after that.

CHAPTER SEVEN

*W*hy did it have to feel so good standing here, wrapped in Collin's arms? Why did he seem to know everything she needed right when she needed it? She took in a quiet breath, breathing in the scent of his cologne and what she could only assume was his natural scent.

It washed over her and her body instantly relaxed. She allowed herself to lean into the hug. Being held was something she missed since being on her own. Sure, she hugged Macie when she was sad or hurt, but sometimes, Quinn just needed someone to hold *her*. To tell her that everything was going to be okay. To help shoulder the responsibility of caring for a tiny human being.

And right now, the fact that it was Collin who was fulfilling that role made her heart beat an erratic rhythm.

He was here. Holding her…but for how long?

Suddenly, fear crept into her heart. Men always left her.

Finding something else that was better than her. Would that happen again?

She shook her head. She was stupid. Of course it would. He was leaving after Christmas. There was nothing that would keep him in this sleepy town. Certainly not her. She couldn't keep him here before, what made her think she could do that now?

So, in an act of self-preservation, she took a step back, wrapping her arms around her chest. She felt so raw from all of the emotions rushing through her.

It had to be Collin's return and the fact that her house was a pile of ash. It couldn't be anything else.

Collin ran his hands through his hair as he kept his gaze on the floor. Then he tipped his face up and gave her a small smile.

"Is there anything I can do to help?" he asked. The depth of his voice sent shivers across her skin.

She pinched her lips together and shook her head. "No. I just have a lot to do."

He studied her, his brows pushed together. Then he reached into his back pocket and started scrolling on his screen. "How about I get someone to help you document all the things you lost?"

Quinn parted her lips and before she could protest, he held the receiver to his cheek.

"Ada?"

A high-pitched voice responded.

Collin glanced at Quinn as he spoke. "I need you on the

next flight to Montana. A good friend needs your incredible organizational skills."

Ada responded and whatever she said, Collin smiled at.

"Great. I'll send Horace to grab you. Text me your flight information and I'll make sure he's there."

A few more words and then goodbyes and Collin was off the phone. He pushed it back into his pocket and peeked over at her.

She stood there, not sure what to say. "Um…" She chewed her lip. "Who's Ada?"

He studied her for a moment before he smiled. "Oh. She's my assistant and best organizer in New York." He made a face as if he suddenly realized what she was saying. "We didn't and won't ever date"—he lowered his voice—"if that's what you are thinking."

Heat flushed her body as Quinn shook her head. "I didn't think that. And you don't have to tell me who you date. It's okay."

He scrubbed a hand over his face before glancing over at her. "I'll tell you if you want to know."

Did she? She'd already spent so many nights when he left thinking about all the wealthy and beautiful women he was dating in the city; she didn't need him to actually confirm any of her thoughts.

So she shook her head. "It's okay. You have your past and I have mine."

Needing to move, she turned and started running her fingers across the bookshelf behind her. How had things changed so suddenly? She went from worrying about what she was going to do with Macie and her house, to worrying about Collin's past. This was ridiculous and she knew that.

She needed to focus on fixing Christmas and the crap-shoot that her life had become. Dwelling on a man who'd broke her heart and confused her was not what she should be thinking about. Besides, hadn't she already cried enough over him?

There was no way she could handle that again.

So she smiled and side-stepped Collin, making her way into the kitchen where she found her daughter sitting at the counter with peanut butter all over her lips. She was on her knees and bouncing in excitement.

Horace was balancing a spoon on his nose. His head was tipped back and his arm outstretched. Macy was clapping and cheering.

Quinn couldn't help the smile that formed on her lips. She'd known Horace back when Collin and her dated. He'd always been quiet and reserved. Especially when Thomas Stewart was around.

But right now, seeing him perform for her daughter, made her so happy. Macie needed this. Both sets of grand-parents spent so much of their time away that she didn't have anyone to influence her.

And that thought scared Quinn.

Pushing away all her fear and worry, she made her way over to the long twelve-person table and sat down on a plush armchair. She'd let Macie finish her lunch with Horace's show. Besides, she said that she would stick around until this evening. She could push off her confusing emotions until then.

Plus, she had phone calls she needed to make. And she welcomed that distraction.

———

After lunch, Quinn and Horace followed Macie out to the living room. Collin was sitting in the far armchair with a book. He looked so…handsome. His dark hair was pushed to the side and his five o'clock shadow made him look more distinguished.

He was no longer that scrawny boy she'd fallen in love with when she was younger. Nope. He was a man now. And that thought made her heart hammer in her chest.

Macie cheered and rushed over to Collin where she climbed up into his lap. He smiled as he set his book down and turned toward her, pulling her up farther.

Macie was telling him that she finished her lunch and that Horace had performed a trick. Quinn couldn't help but stare at their interaction. Her heart swelled at the pure joy that was on Macie's face. She loved people and talking. When she found someone who was willing to put down what they were doing to listen, Macie glommed onto them.

As Quinn studied Collin she realized, he was enjoying Macie's company as much as she was his. It scared and excited her at the same time. What was going to happen to Macie when Collin left? Would her little heart break like every time Ryan left?

Was Quinn going to be able to pick up her daughter's broken heart again?

She needed to stop this. Right now.

"Hey, Macie. Let's decorate. Then mommy needs to get the bows ready for the dance tomorrow." It sounded crazy, but right now, the constance of making bows felt like the only thing to help her stay sane.

Quinn cringed at the thought of trying to figure out how to tie those ridiculously intricate bows that Chardoney wanted.

She'd been pushing them off for fear of the complete failure they'd be. But, she could only delay for so long and then she'd have to face her fear sometime.

Macie nodded and jumped off Collin's lap. After dumping all the contents of the bags onto the couch, they dug into them.

After the lights and tinsel were up, Quinn settled down on the couch to hook the ornaments. Macie was the designated decorator. She would take an ornament from Quinn and then circle the tree a few times before demanding that either Collin or Horace pick her up so she could place it on the perfect branch.

Quinn chuckled softly as she listened to her daughter instruct these two grown men.

The couch shifted as Ruby sat down, drawing Quinn's attention over to her.

Ruby looked tired through her smile. She'd left her wheelchair on the other side of the room and must have walked over to sit next to Quinn.

"Need help?" she asked.

Quinn nodded and moved the package of hooks over so they were between them.

"So, how are things?" Ruby asked after she picked up an ornament and secured the hook. Macie ran over and took it from her.

Quinn stared at the ornament and hook in her hand as the weight of the world pressed down on her. She felt as if she were floundering in this sea of life, never really knowing when she was going to come up for air. Just forcing herself to survive on the oxygen she was rapidly running out of.

"It's…hard." Quinn breathed.

A weathered hand came into view. Ruby's soft and warm fingers enveloped Quinn's. "I'm so sorry, dear. I can only imagine the stress bearing down on you."

Quinn nodded, not sure what to say to that. She wanted to break down. She wanted to be vulnerable. It was exhausting to be this strong. But she couldn't crack. Not when her daughter was depending on her strength.

So she blew out her emotions and smiled. "It's okay. We're surviving. At least I have Macie."

Ruby pulled her hand back to hook another ornament. "What about you, personally? I hear a lot about you as a Mom, but what about you as Quinn? When was the last time you were just…you?"

Quinn studied her hands. She hadn't been Quinn in a long time. She'd been mother, employee, and woman trying to survive. She wasn't sure who Quinn even was.

"It's been a long time," she whispered.

When Ruby didn't respond right away, Quinn glanced over to see that she was studying her.

"It's settled then," Ruby said.

Confused, Quinn furrowed her brow. "What's settled?"

Ruby turned her focus back to the ornament in her lap. She took her time setting the hook and handing it over to Macie. "Collin is going to take you out tonight."

Quinn stared at Ruby. "What?"

"What?" Collin repeated.

Ruby just smiled at the two of them. "Collin is going to take you out tonight," she repeated.

"I am?"

"He is?"

Ruby nodded. "It's time Quinn had something to herself. I'll watch Macie while you two go out." Ruby clasped her hands together. "Oh it will be so fun." She turned to Horace. "Set up a reservation at Cafe Amor for seven, will you?"

Horace nodded and disappeared into the kitchen. Quinn just sat there. She was pretty certain she had a shocked expression on her face but she didn't care. She was trying to process what had just happened.

When she glanced over at Collin, he looked as confused as she felt. When his gaze met hers, he shrugged.

"Is that okay?" he asked.

Pretty sure that Ruby wasn't going to take no for an answer, Quinn just nodded. "I guess." Then she winced. "I have no clothes nice enough for Cafe Amor."

Ruby shook her head. "Not enough of an excuse. I'm

sure Sandra has something you can borrow. Call her." Then Ruby steadied her gaze. "You're not getting out of this. You need a break and we are going to give you one."

Yep. She wasn't going to get out of this.

Quinn gave Ruby a small smile and moved to stand, grabbing her phone from her pocket. After finding Sandra's number, she raised the receiver to her ear.

Two rings later, Sandra's voice filled the silence. "Hey. How's it going?"

Quinn winced, not sure how to answer that question. "It's...going."

Sandra snorted. "Fallen for Collin yet?"

Rolling her eyes, Quinn turned her body away from anyone who could listen in. "Not happening." Then she let out her breath. "I need a dress."

"Ooo, why?"

"Cafe Amor."

There was some sputtering on the other end. When Sandra finished, she said, "Wow. Fancy."

Quinn shrugged. "It's no big deal. So, can you help me out?"

Sandra clicked her tongue. "Let me think..." Right before Quinn scolded her best friend, Sandra chuckled and said, "Of course. I'll be there in an hour."

Quinn thanked her and then hung up the phone. Turning around, she watched what was happening around her. Horace had returned and was hoisting Macie up to place another ornament.

Collin was opening another box of decorations as Ruby

took them out and threaded the hook. To anyone looking in, they seemed to be the quintessential family. And for a moment Quinn allowed herself to think that way. But then, reality hit her like a big, fat Santa.

Besides Macie, this wasn't her family. They never would be. She needed to get that straight in her head right now. Before her already crumbling heart disintegrated for good.

CHAPTER EIGHT

*C*ollin adjusted his tie as he stared at himself in the mirror. What was he doing? Why did he care what he looked like? Every time he tried to get close to Quinn, she pulled away. A constant reminder that he'd hurt her and she was never going to trust him again.

He sighed as he grabbed his cologne and sprayed it. He needed to get his head on straight. This wasn't a date. This wasn't…anything. It was a break for Quinn and he was being selfish if he spent the entire evening trying to get her to reveal her feelings for him…or lack thereof.

And then he felt stupid for trying so hard. Sure, Cafe Amor required black tie formal wear, but he didn't have to care about how he styled his hair or if he was wearing cologne. Should he shower it off? Did he want Quinn to know that he cared?

After a glance at his watch, he cursed under his breath.

He was late. Grabbing his coat, he slipped it on. Then he grabbed his door handle and turned off his light.

He took a deep breath as he stepped out into the hall. He could hear voices coming from downstairs.

He stood in the foyer, glancing around. Macie and Ruby were sipping hot chocolate in the living room, right in front of the tree. They had finished decorating it and turned all the lights off so the twinkling from the tree lights and glitter on the ornaments could be seen.

Macie giggled, causing Collin's heart to swell. He crossed the foyer and leaned against the wall.

As if sensing him, Macie turned. Her eyes widened as she set her cup down and jumped off the chair. She rushed over, lifting her hands out as if she was warning him that she was going to jump.

He laughed and hoisted her up.

When she was eye level, she pulled back. "You look like a prince," she said.

He raised an eyebrow. "I do?"

She leaned from one side to the other, like she was inspecting him. When she came back to center, she nodded. "Yep. You do." Then she leaned toward him. "Will you take me to the dance tomorrow?" Her expression grew sad. "Daddy said he can't come and I don't want to be the only one without their prince."

Emotions choked Collins throat as he studied Macie. Wow. Was this what having a family was like? "You want me to take you?"

She nodded. "Yep."

He blinked a few times. "Of course. I'd love to take you."

She studied him for a moment throwing her arms around his neck and pulling him close. And then, just as quickly as it happened, she pulled away and wiggled so that he'd set her down.

Turning, Collin cleared his throat to compose himself. After a few deep breaths, movement on the stairs caught his attention. Quinn was standing behind him in a black floor length dress. Her hair was pulled back at the base of her neck and curls framed her face.

Her cheeks were pink and she had a look in her eye that told him, she'd been watching. When his gaze met hers, she furrowed her brow. He so desperately wanted to know what she was thinking. Was she upset? Happy?

He swallowed and stepped closer to her.

"Collin," she said, her voice barely a whisper.

He held her gaze, hoping beyond hope that she would see his intentions. He didn't want to hurt her or her daughter. He cared about both of them. So much.

"All right, you two love birds. My work is done. I'm out of here," Sandra's voice broke their connection.

She came bounding down the stairs after placing a kiss on Quinn's cheek. She walked over to Collin and lifted up onto her tip toes and placed a kiss on his cheek. His skin flushed as he glanced down at her.

Sandra held his gaze while whispering, "Take care of my best friend. She's fragile."

All he could do was nod. He wanted to tell Sandra that hurting Quinn was the last thing he wanted to do. He'd done that once and there was no way he was going to do it again. He wasn't going to let Quinn slip through his fingers.

"Promise," he said.

Sandra studied him and then nodded. "I'm out of here." Then she turned to Quinn. "I left a few more outfits on the bed for you."

Quinn had made it down the stairs. She smiled and thanked Sandra. After a final wave, Sandra left, leaving Collin and Quinn alone.

Collin turned his attention to Quinn. It amazed him how every time he looked at her, she took his breath away. He wanted to say everything he was feeling. He wanted her to know that he'd never really gotten over her. That he'd changed and wanted a different life now.

But he was pretty sure that this wasn't the moment for that revelation.

Quinn gave him a weary smile. "Ready?"

He nodded and walked over to the closet where her jacket was hanging. After she called Macie over and kissed her goodnight, Quinn made her way over to him and he helped her with the coat.

He reveled in the feeling of her closeness as he slipped the coat up onto her shoulders. Everything about her surrounded him and muddled his brain. It didn't help that Christmas music was carrying through the house. Or the fact that the lights were all turned down, giving the atmosphere a romantic feel.

Quinn took a step back once her coat was buttoned. Collin tried not to read into that too much. She was ready to go. He focused on that being the reason for her need to distance herself.

"Let's go," he said, leading her through the living room and over to the garage door.

Quinn called one last good night to Macie and shut the door. When they were buckled into his car, he started the engine and pulled out of the driveway.

They rode in silence for a few minutes before she spoke.

"Did you mean that?" she asked. Her voice was barely a whisper.

Collin leaned closer to her. "Mean what?"

She sighed and fiddled with the hem of her coat. "What you said to Macie. That you'll take her to the dance tomorrow?"

He cleared his throat. So she had heard. What did she think? Why would that make her angry? "Um, yeah. Of course. As long as it's okay with you."

When she didn't respond right away, he glanced over at her, worried that he'd made a mistake. Her forehead was furrowed and she looked…grateful.

"That would be amazing. Although, don't feel like you have to," she quickly said.

Collin stopped at a red light and took this time to turn and stare at her. "Why would I feel like I have to? I want to. Macie is the sweetest little girl. She deserves to have a great Christmas." And when Quinn met his gaze he took the moment to add, "And so do you."

She held his gaze until a horn sounded around them.

Glancing up, Collin saw that the light had turned green. He pressed on the gas and waved toward the car behind them.

He praised and cursed the need to break the connection that had been coursing through their interaction. This was all becoming a bit too real. He could feel the tension between them from words that weren't said.

Should he be the one to speak them first? Was he willing to put his heart on the line like that?

He winced as one word floated around in his mind.

Yes.

He wanted to take a chance. After all, once the Christmas season was over, they would move on with their lives. He'd go back to New York and Quinn would stay here. If he wanted to know what she thought about the two of them, he needed to ask now.

He pulled up in front of Cafe Amor twenty minutes later. Their small town only had a diner and they had to go two towns over for anything fancier.

The valet came to the door and pulled it open. After a quick exchange, Collin tucked his ticket into his suit coat and joined Quinn on the sidewalk.

The electricity that had been coursing through them seemed to have died down because Quinn seemed to be keeping a distance from him. Every time he stepped closer, she pulled back.

He tried not to get frustrated by her sudden coolness. Instead, he spoke to the maître'd and followed him to their table.

Just as they moved to sit down, the maître'd held up his hand to stop Collin. Confused, he turned to stare at him.

The maître'd motioned above them. Someone had hung a mistletoe just above their table. Not believing it, Collin glanced over at Quinn who looked as if she didn't believe it either.

"Is that…?" Collin studied the little ball of green foliage. It felt like a strange place to put something like that.

The maître'd nodded. "Mistletoe." And then he leaned in. "As requested."

Collin stared at him. What the heck did *as requested* mean? Did someone ask that the restaurant put it there?

He peered over at Quinn whose cheeks were bright red. He parted his lips as he felt the sudden urge to defend himself. "I didn't…I mean, I would never…" Heat crept up his neck and his shirt felt as if it were choking him.

Quinn just shook her head. "It's okay. This type of thing has Ruby written all over it."

Of course. His meddling grandmother. This was definitely her.

The maître'd glanced between them. "Was this a mistake?"

Quinn smiled. "No. Just…someone who wants something that won't be."

Ouch.

She didn't have to say that. Did she mean it? Were they really finished? Instead of showing how her words affected him, he just smiled and hoped his expression came off as relaxed.

"What she said," he replied to the maître'd.

The man looked as if he'd grown bored. He just shrugged, mumbled something about the pain it was to get it up there, and handed the menus he was holding to the waiter.

Feeling bad, Collin glanced over at Quinn. She was watching the maître'd.

Despite the warning bells, he shrugged. "Maybe we should. After all, it seems like they went through a lot to get that up there."

Stupid. Why did he say that?

Quinn glanced up at the mistletoe and then back to him. She looked worried. "Do you think that's a good idea?"

Well, he'd gone this far, he should just keep going. "Sure. It's not like we've never kissed before." What started out as a joking comment sent daggers through his stomach. Why did he have to bring up their past? Was he stupid?

Quinn looked as if she were torn between what to do. Finally, she sighed. "Sure. One kiss couldn't hurt."

Grateful that she wasn't going to turn him down, he nodded. "It's a small kiss. That's all."

She took a step toward him just as he did the same. Soon, they were inches apart. And then, it became real. He was moments away from kissing Quinn. Moments.

He took a deep breath, hoping that she couldn't hear his pounding heart. He glanced down into her deep brown eyes and instantly lost himself. She was everything he'd ever wanted.

"Thanks," she whispered.

He winked at her. He couldn't help himself. He was going to take this moment to flirt with her. "I haven't kissed you yet."

She shook her head, her skin flushing. "Not about that. About Macie." She chewed her lip as she dropped her gaze for a moment. "She deserves more than I can give her. You've…been perfect with her."

He reached up and brushed his thumb across her cheek. All he wanted to do was touch her. Even though their bodies were close, she felt a million miles away. What could he do to get her to step closer to him?

"She has an amazing mother who would do anything for her. I'd hardly say she's lacking." He caught her gaze and held it. He wanted her to know that he meant everything he said.

He could see the uncertainty there. She seemed to cling to it like it was her life raft and all he wanted her to do was let go of it. He'd be that certainty for her.

"Quinn…" he whispered as he leaned closer to her lips. They were the light and he was a moth. All he wanted was to show her just what she meant to him.

Her eyes widened as he took that moment to press his lips to hers. Electricity shot through his body from that touch. It was everything he had remembered and yet, completely different.

Kissing her had never felt this good or this right back when they were kids. So much had changed between them for the better. They were no longer the inexperienced kids who didn't know what life was.

Instead, they were two lost souls, each having taken their own paths just to end up back here. Together.

Quinn pulled back and stepped toward her chair. "There. I hope Ruby will be satisfied that her meddling paid off," she said.

He studied her, confused by her sudden abruptness. Why was she backing away? She had to have felt the the jolt of feeling from that kiss.

But, not wanting to stand there with his heart in his hands just to be rejected, he nodded and sat.

They ordered their drinks and the waiter said he'd return to take their order.

If sitting in silence had been hard before, it was even harder now. It was easier to think that nothing mattered back when they were just exes. Now, that kiss. He cringed. As good and right as it felt, it had been wrong. So wrong.

He fiddled with his silverware. This was the worst thing possible. He wasn't sure he could live with the uncertainty of where they stood but he also couldn't bring himself to ask.

So, for his sanity and hers, he was going to try very hard to forget that kiss. Even if he had to fake it, preservation was key to surviving this Christmas.

CHAPTER NINE

*C*ollin remained quiet the rest of dinner. Quinn parted her lips multiple times with the intention of asking him what their kiss had meant, but she just couldn't find the words. So, to keep herself safe, she'd decided to push the feelings that had coursed through her to the very back of her mind.

Besides, that was how she survived. Put on a mask and hide just how broken she was. It'd worked in the past. There was no reason why she should change now.

The waiter brought her butter-basted lobster tail and Collin's filet mignon. They ate in silence. Once, she thought that he was going to start a conversation, but he was just taking a sip of his wine.

"Quinn?" a high-pitched voice said, drawing her attention over.

Just her luck, Chardoney was standing there in a dark

blue dress with an exceptionally deep, plunging neckline. Why? Why did this have to happen right now?

"Hey, Chardoney," Quinn said, moving to smile at the woman who drove her crazy.

Chardoney leaned forward and did an obnoxious double cheek kiss. She pulled back and held Quinn's gaze.

"I didn't know you ate here," she said. Then she turned her attention to Collin. "And who's this?" she asked, straightening and extending her hand.

Collin hesitated and then shook her hand. "Collin Stewart."

Chardoney's jaw dropped as she turned her attention back to Quinn. "Stewart, as in Thomas Stewart of Stewart Industries? I didn't know he had a son." She smiled so sickly sweet that it made Quinn's stomach twist.

Collin just nodded. "Yep. I live in New York."

Chardoney motioned around the restaurant. "Then why are you here?"

Collin cleared his throat and glanced over at Quinn. He looked as if he wasn't sure who this woman was or if he should be telling her his life history. Wanting to save him, Quinn leaned forward.

"This is Chardoney. Her daughter goes to school with Macie."

"And is the PTA president." Chardoney flicked her long red hair over her shoulder.

"And is the PTA president," Quinn repeated. Like that title meant to other people as much as it did to Chardoney.

"That reminds me. Are the bows finished? I'd love to pick them up this evening."

Quinn's stomach dropped. She was supposed to do that, but couldn't bring herself to fail at one more thing for her daughter. When she saw Collin part his lips, she shot him a look that she hoped said, drop it. There was no way she wanted Chardoney to know about her house. And she certainly didn't want her pity.

She may not have any material things, but she had her pride.

"We're almost done," Collin said as he reached over the table to grasp Quinn's hand.

Whew. He understood her silent, desperate plea.

Little sparks of electricity pulsed up her arm from his touch. Why did it have to feel so perfect?

"But I had to drag her away for dinner," Collin said, winking at her.

Quinn furrowed her brow but from the intense look in Collin's eyes, she decided to go along with it. "Right. Dinner and then it's back to work."

Chardoney looked a bit disappointed that Quinn hadn't failed at something as she so regularly did. Instead, she smiled and gave a forced chuckle. "Well, don't forget about them. Everyone is expecting this dance to be pure perfection." Then she turned to Collin. "It was nice to meet you, Collin *Stewart*."

Quinn winced at the way she said Stewart. Like it tasted good on her tongue.

"You, too," Collin said and then just as she turned to

walk away, he replied, "I'll see you tomorrow when I come with Macie."

Chardoney wiggled her fingers in a ridiculous wave and made her way back over to her table.

Quinn let out the breath she'd been holding and glanced over at Collin.

"So, that's Chardoney," he said.

Quinn covered her face with her hands and groaned. Collin's genuine laugh actually lightened her mood. When she peeked over her hands, she could see him smiling at her.

"I'm the worst. Why did I ever agree to make bows?"

Collin took a bit of his steak. "Because you're nice."

She sighed. "Or stupid."

He narrowed his eyes as if he were thinking about what she'd just said. "Maybe…"

She playfully kicked him under the table. He winced in a dramatic movement as he leaned down and rubbed his shin.

"Okay, now you're just mean." He winked at her, sending butterflies flittering around in her stomach.

But then his gaze turned serious as he straightened. Now the butterflies were moving for a different reason. What was he going to say? Did she want to know?

"Truth?" he asked. It may have been her imagination, but it sounded as if he were uncertain.

She took a deep breath. Did she want to know the truth? Maybe. "Sure."

"You're an amazing mom. I know I've said it before, but there's nothing you wouldn't do for your daughter." He swallowed. "It's something that a lot of people lack. A parent who takes the time to understand their child. To listen."

From the depths of his gaze, she could tell that his father had really hurt him. She wasn't sure why and she wasn't sure she wanted to know, but she could feel the pain emanating through him.

All of this felt too intimate. Too raw. So, she sighed and smiled, returning to her plate. "Thanks," was all she said.

They finished dinner and Collin paid. They kept their conversation light and surface only. She wasn't ready for the depth that their previous conversation had hinted to.

Sure, maybe eventually they would get to that point where they could be fully honest, but not right now. And she doubted that Christmas had enough magic to fix everything that was broken between them.

Perhaps, if she just held out, she could finish up this holiday season with her hemorrhaging heart intact. If she did, well, that would be a Christmas miracle.

———

Collin pulled his car into the mall's parking lot and into a spot. Quinn glanced over at him, wondering what he was doing.

He unbuckled and motioned toward the sliding doors. "Macie needs Christmas presents."

Feeling like a complete idiot for letting her confusing feelings for Collin get in the way of planning the perfect Christmas for Macie, she nodded as she unbuckled and climbed out of the car. This was ridiculous. How had she let herself become this distracted?

They walked, side by side, into the mall. Quinn couldn't help but feel the closeness of his hand as it swung next to her own. Did he want to hold it as badly as she wanted him to? Was she a complete idiot to think that he might want something more?

His phone rang just as they got inside. He answered it. From what she could make out it was Ada, his assistant. She had just landed. Collin said something about letting Horace know that he should leave. He hung up with Ada and a short conversation later, instructed Horace to go pick her up and hung up with him as well.

He slipped his phone into his pocket and turned to study Quinn. She'd slowed her walking, not quite sure where he wanted to go. All she knew was the numbers in her bank account and they were meager at best. Not really conducive to mall shopping. But she didn't want Collin to know just how broke she really was.

Collin seemed to be waiting for her to take the lead. He glanced around the store windows before turning to meet her gaze. "I've never really shopped for a little girl before, so…" He shoved his hands into his front pockets and shrugged. "Where to?"

Realizing that he wasn't going to be okay with them leaving until they had presents for Macie in hand, Quinn made her way over to the directory and scanned the shops.

"Betty's Toy Barn is a floor up and to the left."

Collin's gaze followed her directions and he nodded. "Perfect. Betty's Toy Barn it is."

Quinn stifled her feelings of embarrassment and moved toward the escalator. She stepped on and Collin got onto the step behind her, bringing him dangerously close to her. She tensed, waiting for him to move, but he didn't. He remained a hairs length away, resting his arm on the belt and looking as if their proximity wasn't affecting him at all.

Not wanting to be the only one who was reading into things, Quinn focused on the stores on the second floor that were now coming into view. Places she couldn't afford to shop in. Ever. She peeked back at Collin. It didn't look as if he were thinking about the hefty prices of the mall stores.

What must that be like?

They got to the end of the escalator and she stepped off. Collin did the same and they walked in silence to the toy store. After stepping inside, Quinn gritted her teeth. She was that much closer to having the awkward conversation about why she was only buying one or two toys for her daughter.

She wanted to give Macie the world, but food and shelter were important as well and what kind of mother would she be if she sacrificed one for the other?

"Did you want to get her a dinosaur set?" Collin's voice broke through her thoughts.

She jumped and glanced over at him. Heat raced across her skin when she realized that she'd been staring at a kiosk full of dinosaurs. Definitely not something Macie was begging for.

She wrapped her arms around her chest and shook her head. "No. Macie's more of a doll girl."

Collin raised his gaze and then waved for her to follow. "I think the aisle decked out in pink would be the perfect place."

Quinn nodded and followed after him.

They stepped into the aisle and Quinn swallowed at the prices. They were like a giant, red, blinking sign that told her she was a terrible mother. Even though Quinn had never been a materialistic person—relationships were always more important than things—her complete inability to provide for her daughter in this way made her feel...helpless.

Collin zeroed in on an American Girl doll. He picked it up and studied it. Even though the price made her want to throw up, she smiled. Never in her life would she have imagined that Collin would be doll shopping.

"What would Macie think of this?"

Panic squeezed Quinn's chest. "I, um...think she would like that a lot." How was she going to be able to tell Mr. I-don't-ever-worry-about-money that she was broke?

"It's a little pricey," she whispered as she turned away and waited.

When he didn't say anything, she peeked over at him. He was studying her in an open way. Like he was trying to figure her out. It was almost laughable. There wasn't much to her. She was a broke, single mom. Her story had been told a million times before.

Then his features softened. "I'm guessing me just saying that I'll pay for it wouldn't make a difference."

It would make a difference, but not in the way she wanted. How would she ever keep up the expectations of her daughter if this Christmas was outlandish and the subsequent ones weren't.

"I'm not sure how I'll be able to explain to Macie how Santa was rich one year, but poor the next." She shook her head and grabbed the box from his hands and set it back on the shelf.

Collin's lips pursed as he studied the doll. "Are you always like this?"

Not sure what he meant, she turned to meet his gaze. "Like what?"

He sighed and scrubbed a hand over his face. "Closed off. Always refusing to let people help you?" He steadied his gaze. "Stubborn?"

Anger sparked in her gut. "I'm not stubborn. I'm realistic. What happens when you leave? How do I explain to Macie how one minute, she's getting expensive Christmas presents and then Dollar Store gifts for every Christmas after that?" She shook her head. "You do this. You come in here, thinking money will buy everything. You don't ever worry about the wake you'll leave."

She grabbed onto her purse strap like it was a life raft. "I can't be the one left behind to pick up the pieces for that little girl. I've done that with Ryan, I can't do that with you."

Her last words left her lips in a whisper. Fearing she'd break down in front of Collin, she moved out of the aisle.

After catching a wandering employee and asking him where the bathroom was, she slipped behind the safety of the door and locked the handle.

She leaned against the bathroom wall and took a deep breath. This whole evening had been a wreck. What was she going to do now? There had been some moments where she felt as if she could stay at the Stewart house for the foreseeable future. But now? She wasn't sure.

Why couldn't life just be more straightforward? Why did it always have to confuse her?

CHAPTER TEN

*C*ollin stood in the doll aisle, staring at the numerous boxes in front of him. His gaze kept slipping back over to the doll that Quinn had refused. It was a dark-haired doll with warm brown eyes. It reminded him of Macie. Which felt weird to think.

Never in his life did he think that he would be standing in a toy store, fighting with a woman about getting her daughter a doll. But, he knew that Macie would love it and it frustrated him that Quinn was so stubborn that she wouldn't allow her daughter a bit of happiness for the holiday season.

He had meant what he said earlier about her being stubborn. It wasn't an anomaly for them. Even when they were dating as teenagers, Quinn would refuse to let him in. Refused to let him help. She was going to do it on her own, even if it killed her.

Frustrated—and with a hint of defiance—Collin picked

up the doll along with the house and horse that sat alongside it, and made his way up the register. He was going to get them for Macie and hopefully, convince Quinn to let him give it to her.

After all, he was a pretty convincing guy.

A pimple-faced teenage stood behind the counter. He was trying to hide his phone behind the register, but wasn't doing a very good job.

Collin set the toys down on the counter and cleared his throat. He needed to get these paid for and hidden before Quinn came back.

The boy looked up and shoved his phone into his pocket. He grabbed the scanner and started ringing them up. "Did you find everything you needed?"

Collin nodded, willing the kid to scan faster. "I did. Hey, I was wondering if you guys offer delivery? I'm…wanting these sent to a specific house on Christmas."

The kid looked up at him. "We're not UPS, you know that, right?"

Collin narrowed his eyes. "Yes, I realize that. I was just wondering if I could pay for delivery." He reached into his wallet and shuffled a few hundreds around. "I could pay two hundred."

The kid sputtered. "Two…hundred? Where do you want them delivered?"

"Ten minutes from here. In Shady Pines."

The cashier glanced around. "I might be able to help you out." Then he narrowed his gaze. "For two hundred."

Collin studied him. "You'll deliver it for me?"

The kid nodded and extended his hand. "Porter James at your service. I can deliver it to you whenever you want." He shrugged as he hit a few buttons on the register. "We're closed tomorrow and my mom's not going anywhere."

Collin knew that he should probably rethink what he was about to do, but he didn't have time. Quinn had to be on her way back any minute. So he took the kid's sweaty hand and shook it. "You have a deal. Deliver it to me on Christmas Day and I'll have two crisp Benjamin's waiting for you." And besides, if Porter decided to keep the dolls, it would most likely make Quinn happy anyway.

Porter looked as if he'd just won the lottery. "Awesome."

Once the items were paid for and securely stowed behind the register, he jotted his address and phone number down on a piece of paper. Just as he handed it over, Quinn came walking up with an arm full of boxes. She avoided his gaze as she dumped them on the counter.

She was upset with him...or herself. He couldn't really tell. But it didn't matter. Right now, he'd go along with her shutting down. Eventually, he'd get her to see his side. It was about Macie's happiness, not her pride. Christmas came around once a year. It they didn't make it special, then what was the point?

The order that Quinn collected came to a third of what Collin had paid. He pretended that he wasn't watching as she pulled out her card and handed it over to Porter. After the receipt was printed and the bag handed over to her, Quinn finally met his gaze.

"Ready?"

He nodded. Just as they made their way out of the store, Porter called out, "See you tomorrow."

Quinn glanced back at him. Collin took that moment to press his finger to his lips. Porter furrowed his brow as he studied Collin. When Quinn glanced back to Collin, he pulled his hand through his hair as if that was what he'd been doing all along. She studied him.

"Er, I mean, see you next time." Porter tried again.

After a confused look between the two of them, Quinn shrugged and called out a soft "Merry Christmas" as she pushed open the door.

They walked in silence out to his car. He opened the trunk and helped her place the bags inside of it. Once everything was secure, he followed her over to the passenger door and pulled on the handle. She gave him an unsure look and then shook her head.

Good. If he were honest with himself, he was getting a little tired of her stubbornness. Sure, he'd been confused and easily persuaded by his father, but he wasn't that same boy anymore. He knew what he wanted. And what he wanted was standing in front of him. If she'd only put her pride down long enough to give him a chance.

He climbed into the driver's seat and started the engine. After putting the car in reverse, he pulled out onto the main road. The soft Christmas music filled the silence. Just as he got comfortable, Quinn spoke up.

"Thanks."

He glanced over at her. She had her hands clasped in her lap and she was staring at the snow-covered ground in front of them. He focused back on the road, not sure what she meant by that.

"For what?" From what he could tell, they had an enjoyable dinner and then he ticked her off at the toy store.

She sighed and rubbed her arms. "For the nice dinner. For letting Macie and I stay at your house." She glanced over at him and he could feel her gaze warm his skin. There was something about the gentleness of her countenance that made his frustration lessen.

"You don't have to thank me. It's the least I can do." He let out his breath as he allowed the meaning and kindness of her words flow through him. She was alone. He needed to remember that. And she had the world on her shoulders. Everything she did, she had to inspect with a microscope. Bad decisions not only affected her, but Macie as well.

Maybe he should take note of her cautiousness and instill that in himself. What would happen to Macie if he left? If Quinn took her away? Up until now, he hadn't really thought about his life after Christmas. Everything around him seemed to be leading up to that moment. What would Macie think if he suddenly left?

And then a fire grew in his heart. He didn't want to leave. Was that bad? He'd loved spending these moments with both of them. Quinn and Macie. It was exactly what he'd been looking for. His flat back in New York sounded cold and lonely. So did his dad's house without Quinn and Macie there.

The last thing he wanted was to lose Quinn again. He'd

SECOND CHANCE MISTLETOE KISSES | 95

been a fool in the past to let her slip through his fingers. He couldn't be that fool again.

He pulled into the garage and turned off the engine. Quinn hesitated and he took that moment to reach out and rest his hand on hers.

"Wait."

Quinn stiffened and from the corner of his eye, he saw her gaze drop down to their hands. The feeling of her soft skin under his sent pulses of electricity up his arm. It took all his strength to not pull her into his arms and never let her go.

"I'm sorry for what happened in the toy store. You're not stubborn. You're cautious and I know why you have to be. You're looking out for Macie. I respect that."

Her posture softened.

"But you don't have to do this alone, you know that, right? I...you should let more people into your life. Let them help you. Macie..." He swallowed. The emotions coated his throat as he thought about that little girl. "She offers something to lost souls like me." And then he braved the pain and met Quinn's gaze. "Just like her mom."

Quinn's eyebrows rose as her lips parted. She looked... confused. Like she wasn't sure what she was supposed to say. Realizing that he may have overstepped, he pulled his hand back and scrubbed his face. He cursed himself. What did he want her to say to that?

That she loved him?

He was a fool to think that was even possible anymore.

He'd hurt her and the last thing she was going to do was open herself up again like that. And he didn't blame her.

"Let's just get through the holidays. Stay in the house. It's good for Ruby to have her here." He cleared his throat. "Don't take her away. Please. After Christmas, you can leave. I'll pay for your stay in a hotel." He met her gaze again and hoped she could see the earnestness in his eyes.

She studied him and then sighed. "Okay. I agree. Macie seems good for Ruby." She fiddled with the strap of her purse. "We can stay until after Christmas."

Collin let out his breath. Good. That was a start. At least his heart wouldn't break every time she mentioned leaving. He'd push that fact to the back of his mind and just focus on the here and now.

He nodded and pulled on the handle. By the time he made his way to the trunk, Quinn was waiting for him. They grabbed out the bags and slammed the trunk closed.

They crept into the kitchen, hoping that Macie was in bed. Horace was sitting at the counter with his spectacles perched on his nose and a book laid out in front of him. He glanced up when they set the bags down in front of him.

"How was dinner?"

Collin nodded. Out of instinct, he reached out and helped Quinn take off her jacket. He tried to ignore the feeling of her soft skin against his fingers. "Good. We stopped by the mall and got presents." He glanced up toward the stairs. "Pumpkin in bed?"

Horace nodded. "And Ms. Mayers is unpacking."

Ada. Right. She was here.

"Great."

Horace slipped off the barstool and took the two coats that Collin was now holding. At first, Collin started to protest, but Horace just shot him a look so Collin handed them over.

Quinn excused herself, saying that she wanted to get out of her dress and into something more comfortable. Collin tugged at his collar and said that was a great idea. He followed her up the stairs.

When they got to the top, Quinn turned suddenly, bumping into Collin's chest. He wrapped his hands around her arms to keep her steady. It was an instinctual move, but the feeling of her so close to him made his stomach lighten.

She peeked up at him, a surprised expression on her face. "I—uh…" She swallowed as if their closeness was doing strange things to her as well. Was it wrong to hope?

"Yes?" he asked. The depth of his tone surprised even him.

"I wanted to say I'm sorry, too." She shifted and not wanting to overstay his welcome, he dropped his hands and fiddled with the garland that now wrapped the bannister next to them.

"For what?"

She was rubbing her arms where he'd just been holding —almost absentmindedly. He smiled, enjoying the fact that he had an effect on her even if she was hell-bent on pretending that he didn't.

"For snapping at you in the toy store. You were just being thoughtful." She took a deep breath and held it. "I may have slight control issues, especially when it comes to Macie. But if you only knew what I went through with Ryan and all the broken promises he made, you'd be hesitant too."

Collin nodded as frustration rolled through him. He knew that disappointment all too well. It was the life he led on a constant basis with his father. His entire childhood was just one disappointment after another. He'd even broken things off with Quinn in hopes that his father would become more active in his life.

At first, his dad was. He made an effort to be there. But just as with anything Collin did, his enthusiasm waned. It had gotten to the point where Collin would go months— almost years—before he saw his father.

And the fact that Ryan was off gallivanting somewhere while his daughter would give anything to be with him was just not acceptable.

Collin gave her a small smile. "I understand."

She chewed her lips as her gaze remained on his face. Then she sighed and turned, grasping onto the door handle of her room.

When she paused, he turned his attention over to her. She peeked over her shoulder. "Thanks, Collin. For everything."

He could tell she meant it. The softness of her gaze matched the tone of her voice. It stirred feelings so deep inside of him, that it was a struggle to keep himself on this side of the hall. All he wanted to do was cross the distance and wrap her up in his arms and kiss her like she was meant to be kissed.

But he didn't. That wasn't what she was asking. She was opening up to him and he was a fool to think it meant anything different.

So he nodded. "You're welcome, Quinn."

She gave him a soft smile and then disappeared into her room.

Now alone, Collin leaned against the banister and let out his breath.

He was in deep trouble.

CHAPTER ELEVEN

The butterflies in Quinn's stomach refused to calm down. Her heart pounded and her hand shook as she twisted her body to reach the zipper of her dress. Everything about what had happened between her and Collin had her mind swimming.

Letting out an exasperated sigh, she straightened. Well, there was no way she was going to be able to get out of this dress without cutting it off. Unless…

Her gaze made its way to the shut door.

Collin.

She could ask him. Would that be wrong?

Feeling stupid, she marched over to the door and opened it. It would only be bad if it meant something—which it didn't.

Right?

She let out a sigh and straightened. It didn't mean anything and it never would. Sure, they'd said they were sorry and admitted they were both wrong, but that didn't mean they lived in the same world.

Collin was all wealth and fancy living. Quinn was paper napkins and cheap shoes. To think that they could coexist together was laughable.

Her feet made no noise as she padded down the hall toward Collin's room. His door was cracked open and she could hear low voices coming from inside. She hesitated before shaking her head and pushing the door the rest of the way open.

A tall, thin, blonde woman was embracing Collin. She had on dark glasses and her hair was pulled back into a bun. Just as Quinn's gaze feel on them, the woman leaned forward and…kissed Collin. On the lips.

Startled, Quinn jumped away from the doorway and out of sight. Her heart pounded in her chest. Was this Ada?

She thought that Collin said she was his assistant, but from what she knew of the corporate world, assistants didn't kiss their bosses.

Embarrassment and frustration coursed through Quinn and she pushed off the wall and slunk back to her room. She felt so completely ridiculous for thinking that there had been anything between herself and Collin.

He liked Macie. That was for sure. But she meant nothing to him. Why had she romanticized that?

After shutting her door, she leaned against it. She tipped her head back and closed her eyes. A hot feeling burned her eyes as tears threatened to escape. How could she have allowed herself to think that they could rekindle what they'd lost so many years ago?

Why was she a fool to hope?

She pushed off the door just as a knock sounded in her room. She took a deep breath, pressed on the bottom of her lids in the hopes that the tears would dissipate and opened the door.

Collin was on the other side, looking as stupidly handsome as ever. He was leaning against the door frame wearing a white t-shirt and reindeer pajama pants. When his gaze fell on her face, his smile widened.

"Hey, you're still dressed."

Too scared that she'd break down, she pinched her lips together and nodded, and then turned to make her way back into the room. She wasn't sure if Collin was going to follow her and she wasn't sure if she wanted him to.

Of course, when she turned, he'd stepped into her room. Great. Her body hadn't gotten the memo that Collin was taken because it was reacting to his mere presence.

"I couldn't reach my zipper," she said quietly. She waved toward her back.

Collin's eyebrows rose. "Um…" He cleared his throat. "Do you need some help?"

Not wanting to spend the rest of her life in this dress, she nodded. "Please."

He stepped closer and she turned so her back was to him. She sucked in a breath as she felt his fingers graze the back of her neck.

He cleared his throat again—causing her to smile. And then she forced the feelings of excitement that settled around her to leave. He was spoken for. She had to remember that.

The feeling of her dress loosening snapped her out of her thoughts. She held onto the front and just as he pulled the zipper to the top of her panties, he stopped.

Neither of them spoke for what felt like an eternity. Quinn wasn't sure what to say. Suddenly, the feelings of his fingers against her shoulder made her shiver.

"I think I'll let you finish the rest of it," he said. His voice was so low that every inch of her body responded.

"Okay," she whispered.

Stepping forward, she turned and raised her gaze to meet his. "Thanks."

He ran his hands through his hair and nodded. "Of course." He cleared his throat again and then smiled up at her. "I'll see you downstairs? We have some bows to make and Ada is dying to talk to you."

At the mention of Ada, reality came crashing down around Quinn. She felt like an idiot and a horrible person, all wrapped up into one.

She forced a smile. "Ada. Right." She met his gaze. "I'm excited to meet her, too."

Collin furrowed his brow as he studied her but then shrugged. "See you downstairs."

She nodded and he pulled the door shut behind him. Quinn changed quickly—into Sandra's tie dyed pajama set and pulled her hair out of the up-do. After running her fingers through it, she fashioned a messy bun at the top of her head and then took a deep breath.

She could do this. If anything, seeing Collin with Ada would help bring her back down to reality. Collin wasn't hers and they certainly weren't dating anymore. She was just here to survive Christmas and then move on with her life.

She and Collin were ancient history and that was how it was going to stay.

Feeling somewhat confident—or so she convinced herself —Quinn made her way down the stairs and into the kitchen.

Ada's bright blue eyes met her and her red lips parted into a huge smile.

"You must be Quinn," she said in a thick French accent. She closed the gap between them and pulled Quinn into a hug.

Quinn stood there, not sure what to do. Then Ada pulled back and kissed each side of Quinn's face.

"It's good to meet you," she said as she pulled back and jutted out her bottom lip. "I heard what happened to your house. I'm so sorry."

Quinn nodded. "Thanks. Yeah, it's been a rough holiday."

Ada turned and grabbed a clipboard on the counter. After removing the pen that was clipped to it, she motioned for Quinn to follow her. "Come, dear. Let's get everything written down so that we can submit it to your insurance agency and this whole nightmare will be over."

Even though Ada had just been kissing Collin minutes

ago, relief flooded through Quinn. She was glad that things were moving forward and having someone here who got the ball rolling helped lessen the stress she felt.

She settled in next to Ada and began rattling off any item she could remember.

———

An hour later, Ada yawned. She'd been writing nonstop since they sat down.

"I think I'll call it a night," she said, clipping the cap back on the pen and standing.

Quinn traced the wood grain of the table with her fingers and nodded. As much as she'd love to go to bed, she still had way too much to do.

Ada pushed in her chair, called a good night out over her shoulder, and disappeared upstairs.

Quinn glanced around the room to study Collin. He had been sitting at the barstool the entire time, fiddling with something on his phone. She wasn't sure what and he didn't seem to want to offer any clue.

Realizing everything she needed to do, she stood and made her way over to the countertop where she'd stashed the bag of ribbon making items from a few days ago. She might as well tackle these monstrosities or Chardoney was going to have her head.

Back at the table, she set out the items and studied them. After a deep sigh, she grabbed her phone and pulled up YouTube.

A figure appeared next to her.

Collin.

He was so close that his arm brushed against hers, sending electricity across her skin. She scolded herself for that reaction and vowed to never touch Collin again.

"So, from what I can tell, you need to start with the right ribbon." He extended his arm out and showed Quinn his screen.

A woman with some extremely high hair was standing in front of a table with a huge bow in front of her. She was walking the viewer through the steps of how to create the same look.

A different set of feelings erupted inside of Quinn. Sure, she'd always been attracted to Collin, but this was different. It was deeper.

He cared. Enough to study how to make ribbons for a daughter that wasn't his and a party he didn't have to go to.

Why?

Why was he acting like this? He had Ada and an amazing life in New York. She had nothing. Absolutely nothing.

A sob choked her throat as she pulled away from Collin and moved over to the counter. There was no way she was going to be able to handle spending another minute around him. Especially when her resolve to keep her distance was melting before her eyes.

"Was that the wrong bow?" Collin asked.

He wasn't touching her, but he'd followed her and was standing so close, she could feel him. Not sure how her voice would sound if she spoke, she just shook her head.

"What is it?"

The pressure of his hand against her shoulder caused her to twitch. She shouldn't be liking this. Not when Ada was upstairs.

The urge to run took over so she twisted her body and made her way over to the table. She fiddled with some of the ribbon, hoping that Collin would take the hint and leave her in peace.

That was a pipe dream. Collin had a determined expression on his face. He wasn't going anywhere.

"Did I do something wrong?"

"How's Ada?" Bring up his girlfriend. That should help cool down the tension in the air.

Collin furrowed his brow. He glanced up to where Ada disappeared. "She's tired. It was a long flight and I caught her just after a long day at the office."

Good. This was good. Quinn wanted to keep this conversation flowing. "Does she not have family around?" Quinn began unwinding the ribbon in preparation for tying.

Collin shrugged and stepped forward to fiddle with a pair of scissors on the table. "She doesn't talk too much about her family. They live back in France." He pulled his hand back and shoved his hands into his front pockets. "She's not really the sentimental type."

Quinn nodded as she measured out what looked to be about twelve inches of a tail and folded the ribbon on itself. The woman had made it look so simple. She could do this.

After some fiddling, instead of looking full and beautiful,

the loops were flat and looked as if someone had sat on the them. She could hear Chardoney's mocking tone in her head as she groaned.

"Here. Let me help," Collin said as he reached out and brushed his fingers against her skin. Warning bells sounded in her mind, but she forced them away. He was just helping, not declaring his love to her. It was all innocent. Right?

He folded the ribbon differently and somehow, his loops looked full and amazing. She scoffed as she watched him flawlessly fix the pathetic ribbon she'd attempted.

When he cut the now tied bow from the spool of ribbon, he smiled over at her. Just that one look and her insides turned to mush.

Great.

"How long have you been dating Ada?" tumbled from her lips.

He studied her as if he were trying to understand what she'd just said. "What?"

She took a deep breath and turned to start unwrapping more ribbon. "Ada. You two. How long have you been dating?" It felt like a simple enough question, why was he acting like she'd asked him in a foreign language.

"I'm not…she's not—we're not dating," he stammered.

Now it was her turn to stare at him. "What? But earlier, upstairs. You two kissed."

He straightened then a look of recognition passed over his face. "She's French. It's a cultural thing." Then he furrowed his brow. "I think…I'll ask her tomorrow."

Quinn watched him try to sort out his thoughts. Then

realization dawned on her. That meant he really was single. That all the guilt that she was carrying around since she saw them was for nothing.

He was available. Which was strange to believe.

Why did her heart have to quicken at that thought?

A small smile spread across Collin's lips. "Is that why you've been acting so weird tonight?"

Quinn scoffed. "Weird? I haven't been acting weird."

Collin's smile grew bigger as he folded his arms and leaned his hip against the table. "You have. You've been acting like I'm a leper or something. Every time I touched you, it was like I had a disease, you'd sprint away so fast."

Quinn rubbed her arms, wishing he'd stop. If he kept down the path he was going, he was going to figure out why she'd acted the way she had.

She was jealous. Because she liked him. And she couldn't have him figuring that out.

"I, um…" She sighed as she dropped her gaze. She didn't know what to say to him anymore. In fact, she was tired of being strong. Of acting like nothing bothered her. And it did. Seeing Collin with another woman bothered her. A lot.

He appeared in her line of vision. She tensed, wondering what he was planning. Was she ready to hear whatever he was about to say?

His hands on her skin sent shockwaves through her body. Every molecule of her being wanted him to bring her close. To hold onto her and never let her go. She wanted to be his so bad it hurt.

"Were you jealous?" he asked, his deep voice equal parts playful and serious.

Quinn shrugged. She could say no. She could. But what good would that do? But then, her head told her to be careful. She needed to tread lightly here. "I was shocked. That's all." She brought her gaze up to meet his, and then cursed herself for doing that. All of her resolve melted under his soft, inviting gaze.

"That's all?" he asked, inching closer to her.

She nodded, but each movement slowly died down until she was just standing there, staring at him. He could see through the wall she'd built up. He knew what she was struggling to say.

"Quinn," he said as he reached up to push an escaping curl behind her ear.

Despite herself, she leaned in to his touch. It was everything she wanted and feared.

"How can I be dating Ada when there is already a perfect woman in my life." He turned his attention back to her, holding her gaze.

Quinn's breath caught in her throat. She wasn't sure what to say to that. "There is?"

He smiled and then got a contemplative look. "Well, two women."

She raised her eyebrows. "Two?"

He leaned closer and out of instinct, she tipped her lips toward his. Deep down, she knew what he was going to say, but she needed to hear it like she needed air to breathe.

SECOND CHANCE MISTLETOE KISSES | 111

"They both stem from the same person." He focused his gaze. "You."

Her heart swelled as she watched him lean closer. His lips moments away from hers. They were going to kiss. This time, for real. No mistletoe and no teenager-charged emotions. Just her and him.

And she was ready.

"Collin—"

He shook his head. "I think we've talked enough." And with that, he closed the gap. He pressed his lips to hers.

In that moment, everything went hazy. All of the worry and fear she'd bottled up all her life melted away from her. She was still the strong, independent woman but being with Collin completed her in ways she couldn't describe.

Collin pulled back and met her gaze. His brow was furrowed, as if he were asking for permission to take it farther. Instead of speaking, she wrapped her hands around his neck and stood on her tiptoes to bring herself closer to him. She was going to show him how okay with this she really was.

The feeling of his warm lips against her own flooded her entire body, making her feel lightheaded. Collin took charge as he moved his hands from her waist to the small of her back and then pulled her against him.

They fell into a rhythm and Quinn forgot everything that had been stressing her before. All she needed was Collin and Macie and right now, she had both.

Through her foggy brain, the sound of a door slamming caused her to pause.

"Did I walk through the door into the past?"

Quinn's heart dropped at the sound of Thomas Stewart's voice.

She pulled back from Collin as embarrassment flushed her entire body. This was not good. Oh, this was not good.

CHAPTER TWELVE

*C*ollin forced himself away from Quinn so that he could look up at his father who was standing in the kitchen. He looked tired but also annoyed. Frustration bubbled up inside of Collin from the way his dad was moving his gaze from Quinn back to Collin.

Having enough of standing under his father's scrutiny, he shoved his hands through his hair. "Hey, Dad. I didn't know you were coming."

Thomas scoffed. "Clearly." His gaze traveled up and down Quinn again.

Collin hated how Quinn wrapped her arms around her chest. She was uncomfortable and trying to protect herself. He didn't blame her. If she found out that Thomas was the real reason that he left, she would never forgive his father. And right now, holding grudges over the past seemed silly.

From the corner of his eye, Collin saw Quinn move over to the table where she started collecting the bow material.

114 | ANNE-MARIE MEYER

He wanted to tell her to stop. That she could remain down here. Thomas didn't threaten him like he used to. Collin would be strong for the both of them.

But Quinn didn't look up to catch his eye and soon she had everything shoved back into her bag and was making her way upstairs.

Once she was gone, Collin turned and glared at his dad. "What was that about?"

Thomas loosened his tie as he turned to the fridge and pulled out a beer. "This is my house, Collin. Or did you forget that? I have a say in who comes and goes." He twisted off the top and took a drink. "What made you think this was a good idea? Getting involved with that girl again."

Anger burned in Collin's gut at his father's words. *That girl.* Of course. His father was only ever going to see Quinn as a girl who was out to get the Stewart fortune. But what his father didn't realize was, Collin didn't need his father's money anymore. And in truth, Collin was beginning to realize that money wasn't everything.

"She needed a place to stay. Her house burned down. Plus, Ruby was lonely. You left her here to rot while you go gallivanting around the world, acting like your family means nothing." Collin set his jaw as he studied Thomas. Never in his life had he been this completely honest with his father. It both frightened him and gave him relief. He was tired of being pushed around by a father who thought he knew everything.

Thomas took another drink, all the while keeping his gaze locked on Collin. The he sighed and set the bottle

SECOND CHANCE MISTLETOE KISSES | 115

next to the sink and grabbed the handle of his suitcase. He made his way over to the master bedroom just off the staircase. "I'm going to bed. We'll discuss this in the morning."

Collin bit back the words he wanted to say. It was probably for the best to just let it go right now. He knew his father had his standards and Quinn didn't live up to them, but Thomas wasn't so heartless that he was going to throw her out on Christmas.

Plus, he had Ruby here to help with the defense. They would work together to convince Thomas.

He took the stairs two at a time. When he reached the top, he made his way to Quinn's room and knocked on the door. He waited and began to wonder if perhaps, she'd fallen asleep.

But, the sound of the door's release caused his heart to pick up speed. The door cracked and Quinn peeked out. Her eyes were puffy and her nose was red.

She'd been crying.

The urge to protect her raced through every molecule of his body. He pressed into the room.

"Collin..." she whispered as she stepped back to allow him in.

Without talking, he reached out and wrapped his arms around her. The feeling of her body pressed against his sent his heart to hammering in his chest. He was going to protect her if it was the last thing he did. She didn't deserve how his father felt about her and he was going to show her that she mattered more to him than she knew.

Quinn fought it at first, but then relaxed. He reveled in the completeness he felt when he was holding her.

She sniffled a few times before pulling away. "I should get these bows finished and then get to bed. I'll be one cranky mommy if I don't get some sleep."

Collin glanced down at her, taking note of the distance she'd put between them. She was pulling away. He could feel it. And he wanted nothing more than to reach out and pull her back.

"Quinn, I—"

She gave him a weak, pleading smile. "Not tonight," she whispered.

Collin pinched his lips as he took in her sloped posture and defeated expression. He wanted to talk to her. He wanted to tell her that what his father said about her didn't matter anymore. If she wanted him to commit, he'd do so. Right now.

But she looked worn out so he just nodded and followed her over to her bed where she'd emptied out the contents of the plastic bag. He grabbed the ribbon and some scissors and sat down.

Quinn joined him and soon, they had ten bows tied and scattering the floor around them. "I think that should be good," Quinn said as she stood and stretched.

Collin nodded as he moved to stand as well. "Perfect." He took one last glance in her direction and smiled. Perhaps they did need a good night's sleep. A lot had happened today and he was ready to take some time to digest it all.

He shot her a smile and she returned it with a soft, tired

one. "Thanks," she said as she followed him over to her door.

Collin turned right before he stepped out into the hall. Quinn must not have anticipated that because she nearly ran into him. Her eyes widened as she glanced up to meet his gaze.

He held it, hoping that she'd see just what she meant to him. That he was ready to put the past behind them and commit. To her and to Macie. Was that what she wanted?

Man, he hoped so.

They stood in silence. Collin hoped that Quinn would break it to tell him what she was feeling before he made a fool of himself. But, she just held the door for him.

"Thanks," she repeated. And then sighed. "For everything. You really went above and beyond what an ex does."

The word *ex* felt like daggers in his chest. Was that how she saw him? It couldn't be. But, like so many things with Quinn, Collin couldn't force her to feel or say what she really wanted to say. That woman was closed up tighter than Fort Knox.

He smiled and stepped out into the hall. She gave him a small wave as she shut the door. Now alone, Collin blew out his breath. Sure, their kiss and this entire evening, hadn't ended like he wanted it to. His father extinguished their fire faster than a gallon of water on a single flame, but he was certain she felt something even if she didn't want to admit it.

He made his way into his room and shut the door. After brushing his teeth and getting into bed, he lay there, staring up at the ceiling. The light of the moon was the only light casting shadows in his room.

Truth was, he couldn't deny how he felt about Quinn. How he'd always felt about her. And if he wanted her, he'd have to take their relationship at her pace. He'd give her the best Christmas possible. He'd show her that he was the man to take care of her and Macie.

Quinn was worth that second chance. If she'd only give it to him.

————

Collin jolted awake the next morning to see Macie standing next to his bed, staring at him. As soon as his gaze met hers, she let out a little cheer.

"You're awake!" she exclaimed.

Collin blinked the sleep from his eyes as he glanced around. It took a moment to get his bearings, but when it finally registered what was happening and what day it was, he gave her a huge smile.

She was dressed in the biggest tutu dress he'd ever seen. It definitely rivaled the ones he'd seen from Disney. Her hair was curled into ringlets.

She looked completely ready for the dance. He glanced over at his clock. What time was it?

Nine.

He'd slept in. Grabbing his covers, he threw them off and moved to stand just as Quinn came walking into his room.

"There you are," she said, walking over to grab Macie's hand. "I told you to let Collin sleep." She shot him an apologetic look. "I'm sorry. She's just...really excited about today."

Collin rubbed his face, trying to wake himself up. "It's okay. I understand."

Macie was trying to break the grasp Quinn had on her. "Let me go, Mommy. I needed to wake my prince so we can go."

Quinn let out an exasperated sigh. "It's not for another four hours, Macie."

Macie jutted out her bottom lip and folded her arms. "I want it to come faster."

Reaching out, Collin motioned for her to come toward him. A huge smile spread across her face as she climbed up onto his bed. Her dress billowed around her.

"This prince needs to take a shower and then I'll be down and you can show me how to dance."

Her eyebrows went up. "You don't know how to dance?"

He pulled a worried look and shook his head. "No. I'm worried I'll step all over your feet."

She giggled as she stuck a foot higher into the air to show her sparkly shoes. "I've got high shoes like Mommy. I think I'll be okay."

Collin dropped his jaw in an exaggerated movement. "Wow. Those are beautiful shoes."

Macie's eyes widened as she nodded. "They are." Then she hopped off the bed and jutted her finger toward the bathroom. "Now go get ready so we can start practicing."

Collin stood, saluted her, and made his way to the bathroom. Just as he passed by Quinn, he brought his gaze up to meet hers. She had a small smile on her lips and she was watching him. Her cheeks blushed when she met his gaze.

"Morning," he said softly.

Quinn nodded and her smile deepened. "Morning."

His heart pounded in his chest as he slipped into the bathroom and turned on the shower. As the water pounded down on him, he let his muscles relax. Today was the day. He was going to confess to Quinn just how deeply he felt for her.

He was going to tell her he was sorry and that he wanted her and Macie. That was it. No amount of money was ever going to make him as happy as being with those two made him.

He was never going to let his father or anyone stand in the way of his happiness again. She was meant to be with him and their love deserved a second chance.

Once he was cleaned and dried, he made his way out into his room where he dressed in his suit and tie. After his shoes were on, he styled his hair and headed out of his room. Soft Christmas music could be heard from the living room.

As Collin made his way down the stairs, he saw Horace's arm outstretched and he was spinning Macie around. She was giggling, her dress billowing out from the spin.

Once he got to the bottom of the stairs, he saw his father sitting in a far chair with a very displeased expression. Ruby sat next to him. Her hands were clasped and she was grinning at Macie.

"That was very beautiful," Ruby exclaimed and Macie took a moment to bow.

Collin cleared his throat and all gazes landed on him. Macie squealed and rushed over to him. She lifted her arms up and jumped. Instinct took hold, and Collin hoisted her up. She wrapped her little arms around his neck and giggled into his ear.

"You look just like they do in the movies," she exclaimed.

His heart soared. He liked that she appreciated how he looked. She certainly made him feel special. He grinned over at her. "Thanks," he said as he set her down.

She nodded and then grabbed his hand and lead him over to the center of the living room. She lifted up her hands and he met them, pulling her closer.

Silent Night started up and Collin glanced down at Macie, waiting for her instructions.

"You step back and I step forward," she said, nodding toward his feet.

Collin did as she said.

"Now, you step forward and I step back," she instructed again.

Soon, they were very slowly making their way around the room. Thomas cleared his throat and stated he needed some coffee and left. Ruby relaxed back in her seat and closed her eyes. She tapped her fingers along with the beat.

Collin smiled down at Macie, who was counting. Her lips were moving with each word. Love for this little girl filled his chest and he reached down and picked her up. He grabbed her hand and extended it out in front of them.

Macie giggled but then shot him a serious look. "This isn't dancing," she said.

Collin shrugged and began spinning with her. "This is my kind of dancing."

Macie threw her head back and laughed. They spun for a few minutes longer before Collin felt as if he was going to be sick. He set her back down and she continued dancing around the room as if not affected by the spin.

Collin paused and took a deep breath.

"I'm going to get a drink," Macie said as she danced toward the kitchen. "I'll be right back."

Quinn stepped into the room just as Macie was leaving. Macie stopped and motioned toward Collin. "Dance with my prince until I get back," she demanded.

Quinn's eyes widened as she studied her daughter's retreating frame. When she looked over at Collin, he shrugged.

"We should do as the princess requests," he said, lifting his arms and motioning for her to come closer.

Quinn hesitated, keeping to the edge of the room. "Do you think that's a good idea?" Her voice was full of worry.

Collin hesitated as he studied the worry lines in her brow or the way her lips tipped down in a frown. She seemed such a stark difference from the warm, relaxed woman yesterday. Not sure how to interpret it, he cleared his throat. "It's just a dance, Quinn."

She dropped her gaze to study her clasped hands. He waited while she seemed to have an internal tug going on inside of her.

"I don't bite," he tried again. Why was she acting like this? He'd thought he'd already broken down this wall she'd placed up around her heart. What had changed?

Finally, she sighed and stepped closer to him. "Okay. You're right. It's just a dance…between friends."

Collin's eyes widened as her words. True, it was nice that she no longer hated him, but they'd been friends a long time ago. That wasn't what he wanted anymore. He wanted *her*.

"Quinn, I—"

She shook her head and slipped her hand into his outstretched one and rested her other hand on his shoulder. "Collin, please." She paused as she looked up to meet his gaze.

He studied her. Why did she look so…scared? What had happened?

"Let's just dance," she said.

His throat constricted from all the words he wanted to say. But from the desperation in her voice, he choked them back and settled on pulling her close. It felt as if she were moving farther and farther away from him and there was nothing he could do about it.

The soft notes of the song faded off and yet, they remained, holding each other and moving ever so slightly around the living room.

Collin closed his eyes as he memorized the feeling of her body next to his and the slight pressure of her hands on his chest. He wanted to commit to memory the way she made him feel in this moment.

The doorbell rang, breaking their connection. Quinn pulled away, keeping her gaze turned to the floor. "Chardoney must be here," she said.

Collin tried hard not to take hope from the way her voice sounded breathy. Like she just might be feeling just as he felt.

As he watched her open the front door, his heart sank. He was losing her and he wasn't sure why.

CHAPTER THIRTEEN

The car ride to the winter dance was quiet. Well, quiet between Quinn and Collin. Macie filled the silence with nonstop chatter about how excited she was about this dance. Then she moved to listing off all the reindeer that she knew and then broke into the *Twelve Days of Christmas* song.

Quinn peeked over at Collin who had his hand on the wheel. His knuckles were white. Like he was fighting an internal battle or something.

She had a feeling as to why he was upset, but she wouldn't allow herself to think about changing her decision. She needed to get out of Thomas Stewart's house. Tonight.

She couldn't allow herself to confuse her place. She wasn't Stewart material. And if she'd deluded herself over these past few days into thinking that she was, Thomas had certainly set her straight this morning before Collin got up.

He didn't say it directly, but she could tell from his questions and the look in his eyes, she wasn't welcomed there. That he doubted her intentions with Collin. Especially when he found out she had a daughter.

She let out her breath slowly as the feelings of inadequacy which Thomas always seemed to create inside her threatened to choke her. She wasn't going to cry over this. Sure, she'd crossed the boundaries she'd set for herself when Collin came back into her life, but she was going to be stronger now.

They were going to do this dance together and then she was calling the Sleepy Motel and setting up a room for her and Macie. She wasn't going to go back to that house with that man. And she couldn't ask Collin to choose between his family and her.

It was better to just leave.

Collin pulled into the parking lot and turned off the engine. He glanced over at her and she could feel his question in his gaze. He was confused and he had every right to be. She just knew that explaining what happened wouldn't make a difference. She and Collin weren't right for each other. They weren't right years ago—and they weren't right now.

"Let's go," she said, faking a smile and turning to open the door. Macie was already out of the car and twirling around the parking lot.

She saw his jaw tighten, but she didn't dwell on it. Instead, she stepped out and stood, calling to Macie to stop dancing she was going to get hit by a car.

Collin stayed a few steps behind them as they made their

way into the school. Quinn forced the knotted feeling in her stomach to loosen as she opened the door and nodded to a few of the PTA moms who lined the hallway.

After showing her tickets, they were waved into the gymnasium where loud Christmas music was blaring from inside.

Quinn checked their coats and then her and Collin followed after Macie who was half-dancing, half-sprinting into the gym.

Quinn's jaw dropped as she saw the decorations. As much as she gave Chardoney a hard time for her insistence on perfection, she really knew how to decorate. She even made Quinn's pathetic bows look professional.

Four tall Christmas trees dotted each corner of the room. They were as tall as the ceiling and perfectly decorated. Streamers hung low on the ceilings with snowflakes ever few inches. Huge presents lined the stage where the DJ was set up. Food tables were fully stocked and parents were happily munching on the goodies.

"This is amazing," Macie breathed out as she glanced up at Quinn. Her eyes were as wide as saucers.

Quinn just nodded and bent down to hug her daughter. Despite the fact that she felt so out of place at the Stewart's house, she still had Macie. And wherever Macie was, she was home. She didn't need her now burned down house or an expensive hotel. She just needed her daughter.

Tears stung her eyes as she squeezed her daughter. Macie giggled and wiggled to get down. "I've gotta dance, mommy," she said.

Quinn held her for a moment longer before setting her down. Macie let out a squeal and when Quinn brought her gaze up to see what Macie was excited about, her stomach sank.

Ryan was walking toward them with a huge grin on his face. She stared, not sure if she was seeing things right.

"Ryan?" she asked as he approached and pulled Macie up into a hug.

Ryan smiled as he squeezed Macie and then set her down. "I wouldn't miss this."

Quinn raised her eyebrows. When it came to her spastic ex, she didn't believe a word he said. "That's not what you said in your text. When you said, *I'm not coming.*" She set her hands on her hips and stared Ryan down.

Ryan just shot her a look and then his gaze moved behind her. Collin stepped into view and extended his hand.

"Collin," Ryan said and they shook.

Collin's gaze moved from Quinn back over to Ryan. "How's it going?"

Ryan nodded. "Good. Just making some time for my girls." Ryan moved to stand next to Quinn and wrapped his arm around her shoulders.

Collin's eyebrows rose and Quinn's muscles tightened. Sure, she didn't want Collin to think that anything could happen between them, but this was not the reason why.

Macie came over and grabbed onto Ryan's hand. "Are you staying for Christmas?" she asked, glancing up to him.

Quinn's stomach twisted at the confusion her daughter must feel. Ryan came into their life and left faster than a heartbeat. She wanted to make sure that he didn't make her any promises that he couldn't keep.

"I am," he said, pulling her up into a hug again.

She squealed and squeezed his neck.

Quinn raised her eyebrows. This was brand new information to her. "You're staying? Where?"

He set her down and Macie ran off to say hi to Serenity. "The Sleepy Motel," he said. "I'm hoping we can spend the holiday together."

Quinn swallowed down the acid that rose in her throat. "I'm—well, we're..."

She didn't know what to say. If Thomas didn't want her in his house, she doubted that he'd be fine with Ryan slumming it there.

Ryan's arm found her shoulders again and he pulled her into a side hug. "Come on. It's not a big deal. You can stay with me."

Quinn stepped away and her gaze found its way over to Collin who looked as if he were trying not to eavesdrop. She wasn't sure what he was thinking. Feeling too overwhelmed by what his expression meant, she focused back on Ryan who'd moved so he could face her.

He sighed. "I know I haven't always been there, but Daisy and I broke up. I...ended it with her. I realized what was most important." He waved his hand toward Macie. "You and Macie. I was a fool to think that I'd be happy without you." He shoved his hands into his front pockets and studied her.

Quinn's lips parted, but she didn't know what to say. How was she supposed to respond to that? "Ryan, I—"

Ryan held up his hand. "Don't make a decision today. Let's spend the holiday together and then go from there." Macie rushed over and grabbed at his wrist until he pulled his hand from his pocket.

"Dance with me, Daddy," she said.

Ryan gave Quinn one more look and then followed after Macie.

Once he was gone, Quinn let out her breath. She watched as Ryan and Macie danced around the gym floor.

Collin's voice was the only thing that pulled her from her thoughts.

"I think I'm going to go," he said. His voice as low and pained.

She snapped her gaze over to him. Realization dawned on her and was confirmed by the anguish she saw in his gaze. "Collin, I…" She blinked. Her emotions rose up in her body and all she wanted to do was cry. How could they ever be something if his father couldn't accept her? Maybe this was all for the best.

Collin shook his head. "It's okay, Quinn. I understand." He studied her for a moment before he reached out and his hand hovered over her own. His gaze dropped to their hands. She tensed anticipating his touch, but it never came.

Instead, he curled his fingers into a fist and dropped his hand. She watched—in slow motion—as he gave her a small smile and turned and then walked toward the door.

She wanted to call out. She wanted to tell him to stop. To

explain herself. But she couldn't. Not when she wasn't sure what she wanted. She'd been strung along by Ryan her whole life and there was no way she wanted to do that to Collin.

If they weren't meant to be, no Christmas spirit or Christmas magic was going to change that. Perhaps it was time that they accepted what they once had and move on.

So, despite the fact that watching him leave was ripping her heart apart, she turned away and focused on her daughter. Macie was happily dancing around Ryan like nothing had happened. Like they were still that small family.

Even though she knew that rekindling something with Ryan would never happen, her happiness didn't matter. Right now, everything was for Macie and she was going to keep it that way.

———

An hour later, Macie stopped dancing, and looked up at Quinn. Her eyes were wide as she glanced around. "Mommy, where did my prince go?"

Quinn stopped moving and studied her daughter. "Collin?"

Macie jutted out her lower lip. "Yes. My prince. Where did he go?"

Quinn dropped down to meet her gaze. "He went home."

Her lip quivered. "Why? Did I do something wrong?" she asked, her voice dropping to a whisper.

Quinn wrapped her daughter up in a hug. "What? No. Of

course not. He just wanted you to have some time with your daddy."

Where had Ryan gone? She straightened to see him coming into the gym talking to...Chardoney. Of course. Not a minute back and he was flirting again. Even if it was completely platonic, it confirmed to Quinn that she could never be anything more than friends with Ryan. Their romance ship had sailed. Far, far away.

A tear rolled down Macie's face. "I miss him. I hope he didn't think I wanted him to go."

Quinn reached out and wiped Macie's cheek. "I don't think he thought that at all." She led Macie over to the tables and sat on a chair that was pulled up next to it. Macie climbed up into her lap and laid her head on Quinn's shoulder. She took a deep breath and fiddled with the material of her dress.

"Mommy?" she asked.

Quinn glanced down. "What my sweet."

"Is Daddy staying here for Christmas?"

Quinn's gaze made its way over to Ryan who was filling a plate full of food. "I think so."

She snuggled in even more. "Good. I asked Santa for Daddy to come." Then she paused. "I think it will be fun to be at Ruby's house with Daddy."

Quinn winced at Macie's assumption. How was she going to tell her daughter that she couldn't stay in the same house as Thomas and Collin? That they were leaving as soon as they got their things.

"We are going to stay at a motel." She pulled back so she

could meet her daughter's gaze. "Won't that be fun? Daddy will be in the room next to us."

Macie's brow furrowed. "Not at Ruby's house?"

Quinn shook her head.

"And my prince?"

Quinn loved and hated the fact that Macie called Collin *her prince*. It just reminded her of how good he was and made her feel like an idiot for walking away from him. "He'll stay at his house. With his family."

Macie's eyes grew wide. "Will Santa know where to find me in the new place?"

Quinn laughed and pulled her daughter back into a hug. "Of course. He knows where all the good little girls are staying."

Macie was quiet as she fiddled with her skirt. "Mommy?"

"Yes?"

"That makes me sad. I want to see my prince on Christmas."

Quinn closed her eyes for a moment. Truth was, so did she. But she was beginning to believe that there wasn't enough Christmas magic in the world to make something like that happen. It was probably best for Macie and certainly best for Quinn to walk away now.

Before it hurt too much to do later.

CHAPTER FOURTEEN

*C*ollin sat in his car that was parked in the garage. His hands were gripping the steering wheel and he was lost in his thoughts. Well, thoughts were stretching it. He was lost in his anger, frustration, and hurt.

He couldn't describe what it felt like to watch Ryan walk up and hug Macie. Or to see her wrap her arms around his neck. Sure, he was her father, but Quinn had said the guy had been MIA more than he was around. And the fact that he could just walk up like that and pretend that nothing was wrong, made Collin's blood boil.

He cared too much about that little girl to let her father treat her like that.

Collin blew out his breath as he stared at the boxes which were stacked on the shelving in front of him. He was an idiot. He should have known when he saw the scratch on his car. He should have kept them at a distance. All of them.

Yet, he let them in. He allowed himself to care for them. And he was hurt.

Badly.

The worst part of it all was, he still cared about both of them. He still wanted them to be happy. To have a fabulous Christmas. He wanted everything for them, even if it didn't include him.

The garage door next to him opened. Collin glanced over his shoulder to see his father's car pull in next to him. Once Thomas got out, he passed by Collin's car just to pause, and peer in through Collin's windshield.

Feeling like an idiot sulking in his car, Collin pulled on the handle and got out.

"What are you doing?" Thomas asked, nodding toward Collin's car.

Not sure what to say, Collin just shrugged.

Thomas raised his eyebrows. "Where's Quinn and her daughter?"

Irritated that his father would even say her name, Collin sighed. "At the school dance. With Ryan."

"That girl's father?"

Collin nodded.

His dad harrumphed. "Good. She should go back to the dad. Leave you out of her mess."

Collin's gaze whipped to his father. Did Thomas just say that? "What's the matter with you?"

Thomas turned to study him. "'What?"

"Are you serious? Sure, Quinn is poor. And she's a single

mother, but she has more gentleness and kindness in her toe than you do your entire body." Collin's body shook with anger. He was done with his father. "I hope I will never become what you've become. I should have never listened to you."

They stood in the middle of the garage staring at each other. Thomas' lips were parted like he wanted to say something.

Collin just shook his head. "I'm no longer living my life for you. If I want Quinn in my life, then she'll be in my life." Collin turned and headed into the house.

The only thing that stung more than his father's opinion of Quinn, was the fact that despite what he said, Quinn wanted nothing to do with him. He was only going to end up more alone this holiday season. But he couldn't allow his father to treat him this way anymore.

Once inside, he kicked off his shoes and made his way into the kitchen. Ada was sitting at the counter typing on her computer.

"Hey. How was the ball?" she asked, giving him a big smile. Then she glanced behind him. "Where are the girls?"

He shrugged and walked over to the fridge and pulled it open. He heard the garage door open and close. Ada greeted Thomas who mumbled something under his breath. Then his footsteps grew faint as he made his way to the stairs.

She returned to typing. "Everything okay? Did you need anything? Can I help?" she asked. She must have felt the tension between them.

Collin shook his head and leaned against the counter as he nursed a beer he'd just opened. "Ruby? Horace? Are they here?" There was no way he wanted to talk about what had just happened. To anyone.

She eyed him. "You're beginning to make me feel like I'm not welcome." She shot him a pointed look. "Sleeping and reading in the living room."

He leaned against the counter, needing to talk to someone. "Quinn and I used to date. A long time ago. But she wasn't good enough for my dad. He threatened to take away my inheritance—the money I was using to go to school—if I didn't break it off with her."

Collin ran his hands through his hair. It felt good and painful to relive his past like this. But he needed to talk this through with someone.

"Okay," she said.

"So I did. I broke it off with the thought that I would come back after I didn't need his money anymore and start things back up again." He blew out his breath and closed his eyes, remembering how it felt to come back just to find out that Quinn was married. "She was married. To this piece of work from high school."

Ada remained quiet, so he continued.

"I left. I never came back. This town held too many bitter memories. But, now she's single with a daughter I adore."

"So what's the problem?" Ada asked.

Collin straightened and met her gaze. "I thought things were great. Last night, our relationship seemed to be progressing. But today, she was cold. Distant. And then at the dance..." His throat constricted, making it hard to speak. Or it could be from the fact that he had already worked out in his mind what he needed to do. Ryan was back wanting to make it work again. How could he stand in the way of that?

Ada raised her eyebrows. "The dance?"

Collin sighed as he finished the last of his beer. "Ryan showed up. He's dumped whichever floozy he was with and wants to make another go at being a family."

Ada scoffed. "Really? He said that?"

Collin studied her. Why was that such a shock to her? "Yeah." Collin scrubbed his face. It didn't matter how he felt about this or what he thought. He saw the pure joy on Macie's face when she saw her father. It was a look that she would never have for him. Ever. "I know what I need to do."

"I doubt that," Ada said with a snort.

Collin whipped his gaze over at her. That was not the response he expected. "What?"

She rested her hand on the counter and drummed it with her fingertips. "You run away, Collin. Always. That's why you left in the first place. You tell yourself it's because of your father, that you'll come back and get Quinn later." She shook her head. "And you were relieved when you found her married to another man. She wouldn't hurt you. Not if you kept your distance."

Frustration boiled up inside of him. That wasn't true. He didn't run away. He left to make their life better, not himself miserable. It frustrated him that Ada would say that. Being without Quinn had been the worst thing he'd ever gone through. And even though he wanted to delude himself into thinking he'd gotten over her, he hadn't.

And after the week he'd shared with her and her daughter, he was pretty sure that he would never get over her. But, there comes a time in a man's life when he needs to decide what's best for the people he loves.

Loves.

He loved Quinn and Macie. More than he could say.

Years apart hadn't diminished those feelings for Quinn despite his hardest efforts. He loved her more now than he did the day he'd left. She was different. He was different. It was as if their pasts had lead them to this moment.

The moment that he was going to have to walk away. If Ryan loved Quinn as much as he did, he would let her be. He would give her and Macie an opportunity to make the family life that was sorely lacking in his own life. He would never wish what he had gone through as a kid on any child —especially not Macie.

He shoved his hands into his front pockets and headed toward the stairs. Ada could go ahead and think what she wanted about him—he knew his heart. He loved Quinn and because of that, he was going to ensure that she was happy. If that meant stepping back to let her try again with Ryan, then he'd do it.

No matter if his heart was breaking in the process.

———

By the time Macie's cheerful voice carried up the stairs and into Collin's bedroom, he'd come up with the perfect plan. After calling around to a few hotels, he booked Ryan and Quinn conjoining luxury suites. The woman on the phone guaranteed that the rooms were each decorated to the hilt in Christmas decorations.

He also pre-paid a month for Quinn. She'd need a place to stay once he was gone and the dingy Sleepy Motel was not conducive for them. He even convinced Ada to stay on for the next week to make sure that Quinn got all the paperwork signed and necessary people contacted.

Now, he needed to let her go.

He winced as he sat up from his bed and swung his feet over the side. He pushed his hands through his hair, hoping that the sour feeling in his stomach would dissipate. He wanted this—well, he wanted this because it was what Quinn wanted. And if he shared his feelings with her now, he'd be asking her to choose. Just like his father had done years ago.

Nope. He was going to step down. Keep the pain that comes from making the wrong choice away from Quinn. She didn't deserve that. Not the day before Christmas Eve.

He made his way down the stairs to find Ryan standing in his foyer. He couldn't help but glare at the man. How much he disliked everything he stood for.

Ryan seemed oblivious to Collin's scowl. Instead, he just grinned as Collin descended the last step and stuck his hand out.

"Good to see you again," he said.

Collin met his handshake and held it for a moment before dropping his hand.

Thankfully, Quinn appeared from behind him wheeling the suitcase that Sandra had brought for her to use. She hesitated as she left it next to Ryan. She raised her gaze—locking it on Collin's.

His heart hammered and the room felt as if it were spinning. What did she want from him? What did she want him to say?

She studied him and then smiled. It seemed small and forced but he only allowed his thoughts to go that far. Dissecting her meaning would not end well for him. It was smarter to just stick to his decision and not falter.

"How was the dance?" he asked.

She furrowed her brow and then sighed. "It was…good." She glanced behind him in the direction of the stairs. "Macie had a fun time. She was asking about her prince though."

His heart soared at the thought of Macie caring about where he was. The smile that grew on his face was from ear to ear. He was going to miss that goofy, heart-melting little girl.

"She did?"

Quinn chewed her lip and nodded. "Yeah." She paused and the electricity that raced through her gaze send shivers up his spine.

He needed to get her out of here before he lost his nerve and bolted the doors shut, stating that she could never leave. Ever.

So he cleared his throat and reached into his back pocket where he'd stashed the hotel information earlier. He handed it to Quinn, who studied it for a moment before taking it and unfolding it.

"What's this?" she asked.

Collin shrugged—a sense of nervousness attacking his resolve. "It's two rooms at the Hilton." He gave her a small smile.

Her eyes widened. "It's what?"

"Two rooms. At the Hilton." He glanced up to Ryan who looked as if he'd just won the lottery. "I got them. For you and Ryan. So you can spend Christmas together."

Quinn's jaw remained dropped as she turned the piece of paper around in her hand. "I, um…I don't know what to say…" Then she met his gaze and the pain inside it was almost palpable. He studied her, trying to figure out what that meant.

Then she extended her hand back to him and shook her head. "I can't take this."

Desperate to finally make the right choice when it came to Quinn, Collin stepped back. "It's yours. I've already paid for a one month stay." He held her gaze. "Please."

"That's really nice of you," Ryan said, stepping up next to Quinn and wrapping his arm around her waist. He pulled her against him and rage built up inside of Collin.

Before Quinn could say anything. Ryan grabbed the piece of paper and tucked in into his front pocket.

Even though it frustrated Collin that Quinn was so resistant to his gesture, he was grateful that she didn't push him more. Instead, she met his gaze one more time before turning and grabbing the railing of the stairs and calling up to Macie.

After a few attempts from both Ryan and Quinn, Macie finally appeared at the top of the stairs. She was hugging a pillow and staring down at them. From where Collin stood, he could see the tears in her eyes.

"But I don't want to go," she said through sobs.

Quinn sighed. In that one movement, Collin could feel her stress emanate around the room. She wasn't happy, but he couldn't quite figure out why.

"If you don't get down here right now, you are going to be in big trouble," Quinn said.

Macie stomped her foot and shook her head. "No."

Quinn let out another exasperated sigh and moved to start climbing the stairs.

Collin reached out and pressed on her arm, hoping to stop her. "I've got this," he said, trying to ignore the jolts of electricity that rushed across his skin from her warmth.

She whipped her gaze over to him. She dropped it for a moment to study his hand, and then returned it. "Okay," she whispered.

Ready to break their connection, Collin took the stairs two at a time. When he got to the top, he grabbed onto Macie and pulled her up. She wrapped her arms around his neck and buried her face into his shoulder.

"Hey. Hey," he said, pulling her closer. "What's the matter?"

She sobbed and pulled back to study him. "I can't go."

He furrowed his brow. "Why not?"

She reached out and placed a hand on each of his cheeks. "I don't want you to be lonely. It's Christmas." Her voice was soft.

His heart squeezed as he forced a calm smile. Why was he letting this little girl go? Why was he being a fool?

He let his gaze drop down to Ryan and Quinn and forced those thoughts from his mind. Because she was never his. She deserved to belong to parents who loved her. He just stood in the way of all that.

"I'll be okay. I have Ruby and Horace."

She sniffed and wiped her nose with the back of her hand. "But...you didn't even have a Christmas tree. How are you going to know about cookies for Santa or singing on Christmas Eve." She gave him a serious look as if not knowing these things was a serious offense.

He chuckled. "Well, now that you told me, I know what to do."

"But...but, there's a lot more."

He pulled her close and held her for a moment before loosening his grasp. "How about, when you get to your hotel, you make a list for me. Have your mom send it over and I'll make sure to do all of them."

Her furrowed brow relaxed a bit as she mulled that information over. "Every last one?"

He nodded. "Every last one."

She wiped the tears from her eyes and nodded. "Okay."

She wiggled to get loose and Collin complied by letting

her down. She moved to start down the stairs but then paused and turned, throwing her arms around his legs.

"I'm going to miss you," she said.

He patted her head as he smiled. He was going to miss this little girl. Probably more that she'd ever know.

"I'll miss you, too," he said as he watched her pull back and head down the stairs.

After their shoes were on, Ryan opened the front door and Quinn scooped Macie up into her arms. He held his breath, waiting to see if she was going to turn around for one final goodbye.

As they made their way through the open door, Collin's heart sank. She wasn't even going to look back.

But, slowly, Quinn and Macie turned. Macie yelled his name and waved followed by rapidly blowing kisses his direction.

Quinn met his gaze for a moment before she gave him a small smile and nodded. It broke his heart to see the two people who had wiggled their way into his life leaving, and there was nothing he could do about it.

Quinn was gone. Again.

CHAPTER FIFTEEN

Quinn sat on the king-sized bed in one of the conjoining rooms, staring at the small sitting area off to the side. A large, perfectly decorated Christmas tree sat in the corner its lights twinkling off the ornaments. She chewed her lip as she allowed her thoughts to wander.

When they got here last night, she was angry.

It wasn't until Collin was handing her the piece of paper with the hotel information on it that she realized that she didn't want to leave. That staying with Collin was what she wanted. What she'd always wanted.

But, he had asked her to leave. Literally, paid to make her go away. And that action hurt more than anything before.

She harrumphed and flung herself back onto the bed to stare up at the ceiling. It was Christmas Eve but no matter how hard she tried to get into the Christmas spirit, it just wasn't there. And this was a problem that a vat of hot chocolate and a mound of marshmallows couldn't fix.

The cartoon Christmas music could be heard from Ryan's room. Macie's occasional cheers caused Quinn's sour mood to lighten just a bit.

"Hang on, I've got to talk to your mommy," Ryan said, his voice growing louder until he was standing in the doorway.

Quinn turned her head to study him. What did he want?

"Can I talk to you?" Ryan asked.

Quinn nodded and pushed herself to sitting. She criss-crossed her legs and motioned for him to join her. Ryan's brow was furrowed and there was a concerned look in his eye. Quinn's stomach sank. She'd seen this look before. It was very similar to the one that he'd given her when he informed her of the affair.

"What?" she asked, wincing at the bite in her tone.

Ryan seemed to pick up on it because his shoulders tightened. "Daisy called."

Quinn quirked an eyebrow. "Daisy? As in your Daisy?"

He nodded and began picking at the comforter. "Yes. She's…" He puffed out his cheeks and then let out his breath slowly. "She's pregnant."

His words hit her like a ton of bricks. But not in the sense that it would have in the past. Instead of gut-wrenching, the news made her sad. Sad for Ryan. Sad for Daisy and the baby. But mostly sad for Macie. She could pretty much guess what he was going to say next.

"I should go back," he said.

Quinn cleared her throat. She called it. "Yeah."

He glanced up at her. "I didn't mean for this to happen."

She just nodded. "I know."

"I'm sorry."

Her gaze made its way to the doorway. Pain filled her chest at the thought of what Macie was going to say. "You don't have to apologize to me, it's her you need to speak to."

Despite the fact that they had Macie together, Quinn could detach herself from Ryan. Macie was the one who was going to be stuck with the pain of her father leaving on Christmas Eve.

Ryan's gaze made its way over to the other room. His jaw clenched as she could see the indecision in his countenance. Hating the fact that Ryan was leaving when he'd just gotten here, Quinn realized that Macie loved her father and promoting a broken relationship between the two of them did more harm than good.

After all, isn't that what Mr. Stewart did to Collin about Quinn? Forcing his son to choose between two things? She wasn't going to do that to Macie. No one wants to be second choice.

"She'll forgive you," Quinn said even though the words felt bitter on her tongue.

Ryan glanced over at her. "She will?"

Quinn nodded. "Yes. She's a strong little girl." But then Quinn held up her hand. "Get your crap together, Ryan. She's sweet now, but at some point, she'll stop letting you in."

Ryan hesitated as he stared off in the direction of the

tree. Then he ran his hands through his hair and nodded. "I know." Then he shrugged. "I'm a screw up."

Quinn chuckled. He was right. "Yeah, but that's the beauty of a new year. You can change."

Ryan cleared his throat as he pushed his hands through his hair. "Thanks, Quinn."

Quinn slipped to the side of the bed and stood, her legs feeling stiff from sitting for so long. "Yeah. It's for Macie. She loves you."

He smiled. "Yeah. I don't deserve it."

"No you don't. But it's there. It's your job to make yourself worthy of it."

"Can I take her out for lunch before I go?"

It hurt Quinn's heart to think about her daughter leaving for the afternoon but she knew that it was important. So she pushed down all the words she wanted to say and just nodded. "Yes."

When Ryan disappeared into the other room, Quinn flopped back down on the bed and sighed. This had definitely been the strangest holiday ever.

————

Three hours later, Quinn straightened in her chair. Four solid knocks sounded again. She glanced down at her watch.

Macie and Ryan were still out, so Quinn was distracting herself with a Hallmark Channel Christmas movie and a box of dark chocolate. Other than Collin, no one else knew that they were here.

She set the candy down on the nightstand and pulled off the blanket she had in her lap and stood. As she passed by the TV, she turned it off.

Taking a deep breath, she peeked into the peephole in the door.

Collin.

Collin was standing on the other side of the door. Next to him was…the cashier from the toy store. Boxes sat next to them.

Confused, Quinn wiped at her mouth to make sure she had no lingering chocolate there and opened the door. When her gaze met Collins, her heart picked up speed.

Hoping to stand her ground and protect her heart, she folded her arms. "What are you doing here?"

Collin glanced behind her. "Is this a bad time?"

She followed his gaze and shook her head. "Ryan and Macie are out."

His face fell. "Oh."

Even though warning bells were going off in her mind, she felt the need to explain. "Yeah. Ryan's leaving for Moose Falls tonight so he's taking her out before he goes."

Collin furrowed his brow. "He is?"

Quinn nodded. "Yep. Apparently, he and Daisy are going to be a family."

Collin parted his lips but didn't speak. "That's…new."

Ready to get this conversation finished and Collin out of

her life again, Quinn focused on the teenager behind him. "So, what are you doing here?"

Collin cleared his throat and looked as if he'd snapped himself out of the trance he had been in a moment ago. "I hope you won't be angry," he started.

Quinn sighed and leaned against the door frame. She had just about enough surprises to last her until next Christmas. "I'm too exhausted to be angry."

Collin waved to the gift boxes next to his feet. "I got Macie some presents."

Quinn's first reaction was to scold him. She'd specifically told him not to buy Macie stuff. But, Ryan was leaving and Quinn was tired of being the bad guy. So she smiled. "That was really kind of you." She stepped back and waved into the room. "You can just leave them under the tree."

Collin nodded to the boy next to him who bent down and scooped up all the boxes and made his way into her hotel room. Collin remained in the hall. His eyebrows were furrowed like he wasn't sure what he was supposed to do.

Quinn eyed him and then motioned inside. "Wanna come in? I can make us some hot chocolate." But the sound of more chocolate made her stomach twist. "Or tea," she added.

Collin hesitated but then nodded. "Yeah. That sounds great." Just as he passed by her, he paused and glanced down at her. "I mean, if you're sure."

The warmth of his body washed over her. It was in this moment that she realized how much she missed having someone alongside her. Ryan was leaving and Collin was leaving. All she had was Macie and even though she loved her daughter, it wasn't enough. She was lonely and her heart was broken.

"Of course," she breathed.

Collin made his way in and over to the small kitchenette where a round table sat just outside of it. The cashier finished setting the presents around the tree and then turned. "Anything else?"

Collin shook his head and stood. He pulled out his wallet and handed some bills over. The boy took it and left, the soft sound of the door shutting marked his departure. The room fell silent just as the electric water kettle whistled. Quinn poured the steaming water into two mugs and moved to set one down in front of Collin.

After setting the different drink mixes in the center of the table, she joined him. They sat in silence for a few seconds, before Collin spoke up.

"I'm an idiot," he said. His voice was low. It sent shivers across her skin.

Turning, she studied him. What was he doing? "Why?"

He ran his finger along the rim of the mug. She tried to calm her heart which was now pounding in her chest.

He shifted a few times on his seat before he brought his gaze back up to study her. "For letting you go."

Now her heart was racing. What was going on? What was he saying? Before she could ask, he continued.

"Quinn, I get scared. I get worried that I'm going to be left. That my heart will always end up broken. I find excuses not to say what I need to say. I convince myself that the people who I love will always be better off without me around." He took a deep breath and hesitated before starting again. "But I'm tired of that. I'm tired of convincing myself that I don't need you. That you're better off without me."

He brought his gaze up and to study her.

She raised her eyebrows, still not believing what he was saying. Did she dare hope what he might mean? "Collin," she whispered.

He held up his hand. "Just, let me say this before I lose my nerve." He picked up his mug and took a sip and then set it back down. "I should have never let my father say the things he did. I should have never allowed him to make the choice for me. I used him as an excuse not to go after you. I told myself it was because you deserve the perfect life and if I couldn't give that to you, then I should walk away."

He sighed, his shoulders rising and then falling. "But I don't need my father's approval anymore and I can more than take care of you. Letting you go was a cowardly move on my part."

He reached across the table and covered her hand with his. Warmth radiated up her arm and exploded in her chest. Every word he was saying was exactly what she wanted to hear.

"Can you ever forgive me?" His gaze met hers and she could feel everything he was trying to say in that one look.

"Are you sure?" She chewed her lip as worry tugged at her mind. She had a complicated life. Macie was a lot to take on.

Hope twinkled in Collin's gaze. He pulled his chair

closer to her so that their knees were touching. He reached out and cupped her cheek with his hand, letting his thumb stroke her skin. She closed her eyes for a second, reveling in his touch.

"Quinn, I'm more sure about this—about you—than I am about anything else in my life. You are the one. The person I'm meant to be with." He leaned closer until his forehead rested against hers. "And Macie is just the whipped cream on top." He pulled back slightly so he could study her. "You are my family. You're the one I'm meant to be with."

He shoved is hand into his pocket and pulled out a small jewelry box. "I know what I want." Opening it up, Quinn gasped.

A princess cut diamond silver banded ring sat in the middle of the velvet box. Quinn's heart hammered in her chest as she glanced up at him. Her lips parted, but she was too shocked to speak.

He shrugged. "Ruby stuffed it into my hand when I left. I guess she really does communicate with fate." Then a calm look passed over his face. "I don't need any more time to learn what I want." He reached up and tucked her hair behind her ear. "I want you, Quinn. Every last bit of you. I'm meant to be with you." He took a deep breath and pushed his chair back and slipped down onto his knee. "Will you marry me?"

Too stunned to speak, she just stared at him. This was everything she'd wanted and yet couldn't believe was actually happening. "Are you sure?" she whispered.

"More than anything else in my life."

"And your dad?"

Collin shrugged. "He'll just have to deal with it. I'm done living my life to please that man. I don't need him making my decisions for me anymore. I did that once and I was miserable." He held the ring up a bit higher.

That was all she needed to hear. That nothing—no matter how hard things were sure to get—would ever get in the way again. She was destined to marry Collin. To love him the rest of her life no matter what.

He was hers.

So she nodded. Slowly at first, but it grew more vigorous as his eyes widened.

"Yes?" he asked, sounding as if he almost didn't believe her.

"Yes," she said, pushing out her hand. He pulled the ring out of the box and slipped it onto her finger.

They stood at the same time. Collin wrapped his arms around her and pulled her up into a kiss. When their lips met, all the pain and worry that she'd been feeling for so long disappeared.

Collin was hers, and hers alone.

She ran her hands across his shoulders and then wrapped her arms around his neck. Collin pressed her closer and spun her a few times. She giggled, throwing her head back.

When he finally stopped, he set her back down and pulled back. He studied her for a moment before leaning forward to press his lips against her nose and then her forehead.

"Love me forever?" he asked.

Quinn snuggled into his chest and let her breath out. "Yes. You?"

She felt his head nod as he rested his chin against her head. "Always."

The sound of knocking drew Quinn away from Collin. He held onto her fingers until the last possible moment before letting her move the rest of the way to the door. She opened it and Macie stood on the other side with a huge grin on her face. Ryan was behind her.

Suddenly nervous about what her daughter was going to say about this change, Quinn moved her left hand behind her.

"Hi, Mommy," Macie said as she came dancing into the room.

Quinn smiled but when Ryan didn't follow, she turned her attention to him.

"I gotta go. I've got a five-hour drive to make and I promised Daisy I'd be there for Christmas Eve."

Quinn held onto the door and nodded. Ryan looked stressed and she allowed herself to feel bad for him. Responsibility had never been a strong point for him so she wanted to encourage it when he tried.

"I'll call next week," he said.

"Yep."

He leaned into the room. "Talk to you later."

Macie had just taken her shoes off so she turned and waved at him. "Bye, Daddy."

Once Ryan was gone, Quinn shut the door and turned back to her daughter. "Guess who's here?"

Macie's eyes widened. "Who?"

Quinn lead her over to the kitchen where Collin was leaning against the wall with a huge smile on his face.

"My prince!" Macie exclaimed, running over and jumping into his arms.

Quinn laughed and walked over. "Careful, Macie."

Macie placed her hands on either side of Collin's cheeks and pressed together so his lips puffed out. "Did you get my note?"

Collin's expression turned serious as he studied her. "It was the best note anyone has ever given me."

Now confused, Quinn stepped up next to them. "What note?"

"I had Daddy send Collin a note where I listed all the Christmas activities he had to do." Then she got a twinkle in her eye. "But I added a drawing."

Quinn's gaze made its way over to Collin who had shifted Macie to one arm and was pulling his phone from his pocket. A few seconds later, he held up a picture that had been texted to him. "I guess Ruby got my number to him somehow. That woman is super sneaky."

Quinn's heart soared. Instead of the picture of her and Macie next to a Christmas tree that had covered the bow-making instructions, there were now three people in the picture. They were standing next to a very dry looking, but well decorated, Christmas tree.

"It's our family," Macie said, reaching out and wrapping her arm around Quinn's neck.

Tears pricked at her eyes as she studied her daughter. "You want us to be a family?"

Macie's gaze moved from Collin and back to Quinn. She got a contemplative look before nodding. "Yep. Collin belongs to us. We can't let him go. He'll be lonely."

Wrapping her arms around Collin and Macie, Quinn stepped toward them. Her heart was so full that she thought she might explode. "I love you both," she whispered.

Macie giggled and Collin just met her gaze. She could feel his affection through the intensity of his gaze.

"I love you, too," he whispered as he wrapped his arm around her.

Quinn let out her breath slowly as she stayed there, wrapped in the arms of the man she'd always loved, and her daughter. Sure, she didn't have a fancy job or a house even. But she had these two. And it was the best Christmas she'd ever had.

EPILOGUE

Six Months Later

"Slow down, Macie," Quinn called as she pushed open her door and raced after her daughter.

Macie didn't seem to want to listen. Instead, she bolted to the brand new, red brick house in front of them.

Their new house.

It had taken a lot of work and finagling with the insurance company, but with the help of Collin, they'd rebuilt and today was moving day.

To say that Macie was excited was an understatement. Months living with Mr. Stewart, even though he promised to be more patient, still had been a trial.

Collin laughed as he came up from behind Quinn and

wrapped his arms around her waist, resting his hand on her stomach. She reveled in the warmth on her stomach where flutterings inside of her reacted to his touch.

Their baby was growing perfectly.

Turning, Quinn wrapped her arms around Collin's neck and pulled him closer. She pressed her lips to his as a feeling of completeness rushed through her.

"How are you my wife?" he asked, steadying his gaze as he met hers.

She grinned and then got a contemplative look. "Well…"

His brow furrowed and she laughed. "I'm perfect, husband."

He smiled. "And the house?"

She turned to study the huge two story house that Collin had helped build. After giving up his busy New York life, he invested in a small building company here and already helped double their workload.

She turned to rest her head on his shoulder. "Perfect."

He pulled her closer as he pressed his lips to the top of her head. "That makes me so happy."

Quinn leaned back to meet his gaze again.

His expression grew serious. "You make me so happy."

She smiled. "I do?"

He brushed his lips against hers. "You and Macie are my whole world."

"And the baby?"

His gaze dipped down to her stomach. "And the baby."

She snuggled into his embrace again. "Good. Cause we aren't going anywhere. You're stuck with us."

"Will you two stop cuddling and help me with my bags?" Ruby's voice broke through their moment.

Collin scoffed and Quinn laughed. They'd arranged for Ruby to spend the time with them when Mr. Stewart left town.

"Granny!" Macie yelled as she rushed over and wrapped her arms around Ruby.

"My sweet girl," she said, dipping down to hug her. She'd had more strength lately ever since the doctors said her cancer was in remission. They knew it was only a delay in what was inevitably going to happen, but right now, she'd take it.

Horace rounded the car, holding three suitcases. He looked different ever since he turned in his suits for fun sweaters and jeans. Apparently, Ruby had worn him down in more ways than one and they fell in love. The wedding was planned for next month, in the backyard.

Quinn snuggled into Collin's embrace as she watched her daughter help Horace drag Ruby's luggage into the front door. Never in her life did she think that she could possibly be this happy.

As her heart swelled with love, she let out a sigh.

"Happy?" Collin whispered into her ear.

She nodded. "Happy."

"Love me forever?" he asked as he leaned closer and kissed her cheek.

"And beyond."

***

Want more Anne-Marie Meyer romances? Head on over and grab you next read HERE.

For a full reading order of Anne-Marie's books, you can find them HERE.

Made in the USA
Monee, IL
07 January 2024

50800527R00097